W9-ALJ-512

"What are you so afraid of?" Dimitri asked.

It was the softness of his voice in the darkened room that undid Anna. In the deepest reaches of her heart, she knew what it was. She knew that she was terrified that she wouldn't just be giving her body to Dimitri, but more—her heart.

But the words wouldn't come. Some innate sense of self-protection prevented her from revealing such a weakness. She looked up at him, swathed in the shadows of the room, marveling at how the light from the moon cast him in silver finery, lighting the sharp angles of his face, making his dark eyes seem to almost glow. He was stunning, powerful...irresistible.

If she'd thought he'd turn away from her silence, she was wrong.

Instead, he pressed closer to her, crowding her, tempting her.

"Ask for what you want, Anna. It is your right."

"As your wife?" she spat at him, desperate to cling to anything she could use to maintain the barriers she had put around her heart three years before, longer even.

"No. *Theos*," he growled. "As a *woman*."

Pippa Roscoe lives in Norfolk near her family and makes daily promises to herself that *this* is the day she'll leave the computer to take a long walk in the countryside. She can't remember a time when she wasn't dreaming about handsome heroes and innocent heroines. Totally her mother's fault, of course—she gave Pippa her first romance to read at the age of seven! She is inconceivably happy that she gets to share those daydreams with you all. Follow her on Twitter, @PippaRoscoe.

Books by Pippa Roscoe

Harlequin Presents

Conquering His Virgin Queen

The Winners' Circle
A Ring to Take His Revenge

Visit the Author Profile page
at Harlequin.com for more titles.

Pippa Roscoe

CLAIMED FOR THE GREEK'S CHILD

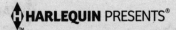

♦ HARLEQUIN PRESENTS®

If you purchased this book without a cover you should be aware
that this book is stolen property. It was reported as "unsold and
destroyed" to the publisher, and neither the author nor the
publisher has received any payment for this "stripped book."

Recycling programs
for this product may
not exist in your area.

ISBN-13: 978-1-335-47810-8

Claimed for the Greek's Child

First North American publication 2019

Copyright © 2019 by Pippa Roscoe

All rights reserved. Except for use in any review, the reproduction or
utilization of this work in whole or in part in any form by any electronic,
mechanical or other means, now known or hereafter invented, including
xerography, photocopying and recording, or in any information storage
or retrieval system, is forbidden without the written permission of the
publisher, Harlequin Enterprises Limited, 22 Adelaide St. West, 40th Floor,
Toronto, Ontario M5H 4E3, Canada.

This is a work of fiction. Names, characters, places and incidents are
either the product of the author's imagination or are used fictitiously,
and any resemblance to actual persons, living or dead, business
establishments, events or locales is entirely coincidental.

This edition published by arrangement with Harlequin Books S.A.

For questions and comments about the quality of this book,
please contact us at CustomerService@Harlequin.com.

® and TM are trademarks of Harlequin Enterprises Limited or its
corporate affiliates. Trademarks indicated with ® are registered in the
United States Patent and Trademark Office, the Canadian Intellectual
Property Office and in other countries.

Printed in U.S.A.

CLAIMED FOR THE GREEK'S CHILD

For Laurie,

who put up with me in New York for six weeks while I disappeared off to my writing table on the roof of our apartment at stupid o'clock in the morning, my rocket fuel coffee, a fan instead of air-conditioning and a dental crisis!

Although Pin Up Girl cocktails, an American football game, incredible food, a trip to Boston and Christmas decorations at Macy's hopefully made up for it!

New York, or this book, wouldn't have been the same without you. Xx

PROLOGUE

Three years ago

'MR KYRIAKOU? WE'LL be landing in about twenty minutes.'

Dimitri gave a curt nod to the stewardess on board the Kyriakou Bank's private jet. He wasn't capable of more than that. His jaw was clenched so tightly it would have taken a crowbar to pry it open. The only thing that had successfully passed his lips since his boarding the plane had been a whisky. Only one. That was all he would allow himself.

He glanced out of the window and, although he should have been seeing the soft white clouds that hovered above the English Channel, instead he saw the slope of a beautiful woman's shoulder. Naked, exposed…vulnerable. Beneath the palm of his hand he could feel the silky texture of her skin. His fingers twitched at the memory.

He ran a hand across his face, rubbing at the exhaustion of the last year, allowing the stubble of his jaw to scratch at the itch that made him want to turn the plane around. To go back to the bed where the beautiful woman lay—probably still asleep. He'd snuck out like a thief. An analogy that caught in the back of his throat, and for an awful moment he thought he might actually choke.

He couldn't fathom what he'd been thinking. But that was the problem. He *hadn't* been. Despite the knowledge that this day had been coming, the knowledge of exactly what would greet him the moment the plane touched down in the States, Dimitri had needed one night. Just one night...

Yesterday, he'd left Antonio Arcuri and Danyl Nejem Al Arain—his best friends and fellow members of the Winners' Circle Racing Syndicate—behind at the Dublin Race Series and allowed instinct to take over. As he'd slid into the driver's seat of the powerful black supercar the thrust of the engine met the need for freedom coursing through his veins. He'd followed the road out of the small city, past the huge doors of the Guinness brewery, through dark streets, along roads that slowly found their way into rolling green countryside. It was only then that he'd felt able to breathe. Only then that he'd been able to block out what was to come.

Unconsciously he'd manoeuvred the sleek, dark car down impossibly windy roads, allowing only the thrill of the powerful machine beneath him to fill his senses. Something was driving him—he wasn't willing to give it a name.

Dimitri had slowed only when the car's petrol light came on. He'd found himself in a small village and, if it had had a name, he hadn't noticed. An old pub with a black sign and peeling paint defiantly stared down an even older church at the opposite end of the one street that divided the village. He followed the road to the end, where, instead of finding a petrol station, he came to a large gravel drive in front of a small bed and breakfast.

To Dimitri the Irish were known for two things: hospitality and whisky. And he was in great need of both. As he turned off the ignition he was hit with a wave of exhaustion so intense he wasn't entirely sure that he could make it out of the car. He sat back and pressed his head angrily into the back of the seat. He'd run and he hated himself for it. All this time, this planning… Frustration at the shame he was about to bring to Antonio and Danyl… It hurt Dimitri in a way he hadn't imagined, hadn't thought possible after all he'd endured in his thirty-three years.

He allowed that anger to propel him from the car and over to the door of the bed and breakfast, the sound of his fist pounding on the door jarring even to his own ears. He glanced at his watch for the first time in what felt like hours and was surprised to find that it was so late. Perhaps the proprietor was asleep. He looked back to the car, wondering how much further it would get, wondering whether he should turn back, when the door opened.

The moment he caught her large green eyes looking up at him he knew he was doomed.

She let him in, quietly, one finger to her lips and the other hand making a 'gently, gently' motion. She beckoned him through to a small seating area decorated with just about everything that he'd expected a small Irish bed and breakfast to have, but his gaze narrowed on the small wooden, clearly well-stocked bar.

'You're after a room?' she almost whispered.

Was he?

'Just for the night.'

Her eyes assessed him, but not in the sexual way he was used to from beautiful women. It was as if she were doing mathematics—on his expensive clothes, a watch that was probably worth half a yearly intake for this place, the car outside. He wasn't offended.

Dimitri took out his wallet and removed all the euros he had in it. What did it matter to him? He couldn't take them where he was going. He placed the thick bundle of notes on the bar.

'No, sir. That's not…that's not necessary. It'll be sixty euros for the night, an extra five if you'd like breakfast.'

The Irish lilt to her voice was a little surprising to him. Her skin wasn't the light, freckled complexion that had populated the racecourse back in Dublin—it was closer to his own Greek colouring, only without the benefit of the sun she seemed pale. For a moment he allowed himself to imagine this woman on a Greek island, sun-kissed and glorious, the sun's rays deepening the natural promise of her skin tone. Long, dark tendrils of hair had been swept up into a messy ponytail that should have made her look young, rather than chaotically beautiful. Loose tendrils from a grown-out fringe played along her jawline, accentuating her cheekbones and contrasting with the lighter golden tones in hauntingly emerald-coloured eyes.

Forcing his attention away from her, he looked at the bottles behind the bar. Scanning them, he was slightly disappointed. If he'd had a choice, none of them would have been it. But beggars couldn't be choosers.

'No breakfast. But I'll take a bottle of your best whisky.'

Again, her eyes were quick and assessing. Not calculating. That was it. That was what was different about her. There wasn't anything selfish in her gaze, nothing judgemental. She was simply trying to figure him out. As if making up her mind, she slipped behind the small bar, not even looking at the obscene amount of money she was yet to touch, and she pulled down two cut crystal glasses housed in a hidden shelf above the counter. The way she resolutely ignored the money made him wonder if he'd offended her and a shadow of guilt stirred within him.

She placed the two glasses on the wooden bar top, waiting for his reaction, to see if he would object to her joining him. It was his turn to assess. She'd barely said two words to him. She looked to be in her early twenties. The white shirt she wore as a uniform was ill-fitting, as if made for someone bigger than her. The worn name tag sewn onto the shirt pocket said 'Mary Moore'. She didn't look much like a Mary. But he skimmed over these small details in preference of one: there was something behind her eyes. Something that called to him.

He nodded, allowing her to proceed. Instead of reaching for one of the bottles behind her, she bent beneath the bar and pulled out one that was more expensive. The good stuff saved for special occasions. Well, he supposed this *was* a special occasion.

She poured the amber liquid into each glass and, when finished, pushed one glass towards him and picked up the other.

'*Sláinte,*' she had said.

'*Yamas,*' he'd replied.

And they both drank deeply.

The plane banked to the right as it prepared to come in to land. Whether it was the drink from the night before, or the one from two hours ago, he could still taste whisky on his tongue, he could still taste *her*. As the plane descended towards the runway, images flashed through his mind. The first taste of her lips, the feel of her heart beating beneath the palm of his hand, her perfect breasts, her thigh as he moved it apart from the other. The feel of her wrapped around him and her thrilled cry as he sank deeply into her. The ecstasy he found as they climaxed together, swathed in each other. The memory of the scream he'd silenced with an impassioned kiss was drowned out by the roar of the backward thrust of the small jet engine as they came in to land at JFK.

Even the air stewardess seemed reluctant to open the cabin door. Her smile was sad as he disembarked, as if she too knew what was about to happen. But she couldn't. Only he, and perhaps two others in the whole world, did—the lead investigator, and whoever it was who had *really* perpetrated the crime.

At the bottom of the small metal steps stood about twenty men in blue windbreakers with yellow initials marking them to be FBI agents. Gun belts with handcuffs and batons carefully held in place sat heavily around each man's waist.

He stepped down towards the tarmac. Looking straight into the eyes of the lead agent, Dimitri Kyriakou, international billionaire, held out his hands before him—as he'd seen done in movies, as he'd known he would have to do long before this flight, long before last night—and as the steel handcuffs were clasped around his wrists he forced his head to remain high.

CHAPTER ONE

Present day

Dear Dimitri,
Today you found me.

DIMITRI GUIDED THE car down roads he'd travelled only once before. Headlights pierced the night, picking out slanting sheets of rain and wet shrubs lining the road. His mind's eye, however, ran through images of his now very much *ex*-assistant's horrified face as words like 'Sorry', 'I didn't know' and 'It was for the best…for the Kyriakou Bank' stuttered from the man's lips.

Fury pounded through Dimitri's veins. How had this happened? *How?*

In the nineteen months since his release from that godforsaken American prison, he'd sweated blood and tears to try and find the culprit responsible for setting him up to take the fall for one of the most notorious banking frauds of the last decade. Not only that, but also to bring his—*his father's*—family-owned bank back to its former glory.

And finally, one month ago, after the arrest of his half-brother, Manos, he'd thought all his troubles had ended. He'd thought he could put everything behind him and focus on the future. He thought he'd be finally able to breathe.

Until he'd received notification of unusual activity on a small personal account he'd not looked at in years. He'd set up the alerts the moment he'd resumed his position on the board of governors and had hoped that he'd never receive one.

But two days ago he had.

And he'd been horrified to discover that, unbeknownst to him, his assistant had arranged payment to a woman who had claimed Dimitri had a daughter. It had happened before, false accusations seeking to capitalise on his sudden unwelcome and erroneous notoriety after his arrest, demands for impossible amounts of money from scam artists. But this time…

Was it some perverse twist of fate that this discovery had coincided with the second leg of the Hanley Cup? That he should be drawn back to Dublin not only for the Winners' Circle, but also because his assistant had transferred the ridiculous sum of fifty thousand euros to a money-grabbing gold-digger who had—

The sound of his phone ringing cut through his thoughts like a knife.

'Kyriakou,' he said into the speaker set in the car.

'Sir, I have the information you…for…'

'Yes?'

'It's…rush… So I cannot guarantee…disclosure.'

'You're breaking up, Michael. The signal out here is terrible,' Dimitri growled, his frustration with this whole mess increasing. 'Can you hear me?'

'Yes, sir… Just about.'

'Look, you can email me the file and I'll look at it later, but for now, just top-line thoughts will do.'

'Mary Moore…years old… One daughter—Anna, no father on the…certificate. Arrests for drunk and disorderly…disturbing the peace.'

Dimitri let out a curse. He couldn't believe it. The woman who had come apart in his arms was a drunk? Had a criminal record? *Dammit.*

'Okay. I've heard enough. Get me your invoice and I'll ensure the payment is—'

'Wait, sir, there's…you need…'

'The signal's breaking up now. I'll read the full file when I can access emails.'

With that, Dimitri ended the call, not taking his eyes from the road once. If he thought he'd been angry before, it was nothing compared to the fury now burning through his veins. He glanced at the man sitting silently in the passenger seat of the car—the only man outside of the Winners' Circle he trusted. David Owen had been his lawyer for over eighteen years.

'Legally, at this moment, there's actually very little you can do,' David said without making eye contact. 'All you have is the request for fifty thousand euros and a grainy black and white photo of a little girl.'

And it had been enough. Enough for Dimitri to

recognise that the little girl was his. He'd looked exactly the same at her age—thick, dark, curly hair, and something indescribably haunted about her large brown eyes. Dimitri acknowledged that that might have been fanciful on his part. But surely, with an alcoholic criminal as a mother, that was a given.

'You have no actual proof that the child is yours.'

'I don't need it. I know it. *Know* that she is my blood. The timing fits, and, *Theos*, David, you read the email, you saw that picture too.'

David nodded his head reluctantly. 'We could engage Social Services, but that would cause publicity and scandal.'

'No. I will not have any more scandal attached to the Kyriakou name. Besides, it would take too long. The reason you're here is to help me get what I want without any of that. I can't afford for the press to find out about this yet. The mother is clearly only in it for the money. A little legal jargon will help grease the wheels, so to speak.'

The satnav on his phone told him to take the next left. How on earth Dimitri had found his way to that little bed and breakfast three years before, he had no idea.

'Are you sure you want to do this? As I said, legally your position is not the strongest.'

'She lost her right to any legal standing when she tried to blackmail me,' Dimitri bit out.

How could he have been so deceived? *Again?* How could he have let that happen?

Throughout his wrongful imprisonment, fourteen months incarcerated and locked behind bars like an animal, he'd held up the memory of that one night, of *her*, as a shining beacon in the darkness. A moment completely for him, known only to them. He'd lived off the sounds of her pleasure, the cries of ecstasy and that first, single moment—the moment when he'd been shocked, and ever so secretly pleased, to find that she had been a virgin—he'd drawn it deep within him, hugged it to him and allowed it to get him through the worst of the time he'd spent in prison.

Had he been deceived by her innocence? Had she *really* been a virgin? But even he had to acknowledge that thought as inherently wrong. It may have been the only true thing about Mary Moore. But the rest? She'd lied. She'd kept a secret from him. And she'd live to regret it for the rest of her life. Because nothing would prevent him from claiming his child.

Anna gasped as the rain pelted down even harder. It snuck beneath the neck of the waterproof jacket she'd slung around her shoulders the moment she got the phone call. She hadn't had the presence of mind to bring an umbrella though. She dug her hand into the pocket and pulled out the only protection she had with her against the elements. And the irony of that was enough to poke and prod at the miserable situation she was in.

She pulled the large, thin envelope from her pocket and held it over her head as the paper ate up the rain in seconds, and water dripped down her jacket sleeve and arm, to eagerly soak the cotton of her T-shirt.

It didn't matter if the letter got wet. She knew it word for word by now.

We regret to inform you...owing to late payments...as per the mortgage terms...right to repossess...

She was about to lose the small bed and breakfast she'd inherited from her grandmother, the place where both she and her mother had been born and had grown up. It might never have been the future that she had imagined for herself, but it was the only one she could cling to in order to support her child. How had her mother managed to keep this from her? Mary Moore was barely functioning as it was. But— Anna supposed—that was the beauty of being an alcoholic. Even in her worst state, her mother managed to hide, conceal, lie.

Through the pounding of the rain, Anna could hear the raucous sounds of music and shouts coming from the only building with signs of life on the road. Light bled out from the frosted windows, barely illuminating the wet benches in the courtyard. Anna braced herself for what was guaranteed to be a pretty bloody sight.

She pushed open the door to the pub, and the men at the bar stopped talking and turned to stare. They always stared. The colour of her skin—the only thing her Vietnamese father had left her with after abandoning them before her birth—had always marked her as an outsider, as a reminder of her mother's shame. She shook out the letter, put the sodden paper back into her pocket and ran a hand through her hair to release the clusters of raindrops still clinging to the fine strands. The smell of warm beer and stale cigarettes defiantly smoked even after the ban hung heavy on the air.

She locked eyes with the owner, who stared back almost insolently.

'Why did you serve her?' Anna demanded.

The owner shrugged. 'She had the money.' As if in consolation, Eamon nodded in the direction of the snug.

She could hear sniggers coming from the men who had turned their backs to her and anger pooled low in her stomach. It was a hot, fiery thing that moved like a snake and bit like one too.

'What, you've never seen a drunk woman before?' she demanded of the room.

'She's not a woman, she's a—'

'Say that word and I'll—'

'That's enough,' Eamon interrupted, though whether for Anna's sake or for his peace and quiet, she couldn't tell.

She stepped through to the snug. Her mother was sitting alone in the empty room, surrounded by round wooden tables. She looked impossibly small, and in front of her, next to a newspaper, was a short glass filled with clear liquid—probably vodka. Anna hoped for vodka; gin always made it harder. She took a seat next to her and pushed down her mounting frustration. Anger never helped this situation.

Mary looked worse than the last time she'd seen her. From the day Amalia was born, Anna knew she couldn't allow Mary to continue to live with them. She wouldn't take the risk that her drunken outbursts could harm her daughter. She'd arranged for her mother to live with one of the only family friends Mary Moore had left. And their exchanges ever since had been loaded and painful.

'What happened, Ma? Where did the money come from?' Anna hated the sadness in her voice.

'I thought I'd be able to pay off some of the mortgage… I thought…just one drink… I thought…'

'Thought what, Ma?' Anna couldn't imagine what her mother was talking about, but she was used to the circulatory nature of conversations when she was in this state. The small flame of hope she'd nursed in the last few weeks as her mother had stayed sober and even talked of rehab spluttered out and died on a gasp.

'Even when he got out of prison, I thought he was guilty…but when they arrested his brother…'

Oh, God. She was talking about Dimitri.

Her mother nudged at the newspaper. Beside the main article was coverage of the forthcoming Dublin Horse Race, with a black and white picture of three men celebrating a win in Buenos Aires. Her eyes couldn't help but be drawn straight to one man: Dimitri Kyriakou.

'And he has all that money…so…' Mary Moore's words were beginning to slur a little around the edges. 'So I did what you never had the courage to do.'

'What did you do, Ma?'

'A father should provide for his child.'

A million thoughts shouted in her mind. She, more than anyone, knew the truth of her mother's statement. But she *had* tried to garner his support… she *had* tried to tell him once about his daughter: nineteen months ago, on the day she, along with the rest of the world, discovered his innocence. She'd called his office and had been met with a response that proved to her that the man she'd spent one reckless night with, the man to whom she had given so much of herself, her *true* self, had been a figment of her fevered imagination.

'Ma?'

'At least you picked one with money…he was willing to pay fifty thousand euros in exchange for our silence.'

Sickness rose in Anna's stomach. Pure, unadulterated nausea.

'Jesus, Ma—'

The slap came out of nowhere.

Hard, more than stinging. Anna's head rang and the buzzing in her ears momentarily drowned out the shock.

'Do *not* take His name in vain, Anna Moore.'

In that one strike, years and years of loneliness, anger and frustration rose within Anna. She locked

eyes with her mother and watched the righteous indignation turn to guilt and misery.

'Oh, Anna, I'm so—'

'Stop.'

'Anna—'

'No.' Anna put her hand up, knowing what her ma
would say, knowing the cycle of begging, pleading
and justification that would follow. But she couldn't
let it happen this time.

Had Dimitri really paid a sum of money to reject
their daughter? A hurt so deep it felt endless opened
up in her heart. The ache was much stronger than
the throbbing in her cheek.

Anna rubbed her chest with the palm of her hand,
trying to soothe the pain that she knew she would
feel for days, possibly even years. *This* was what
she'd wanted to avoid for her daughter—the sting of
rejection, the feeling of being unwanted…unloved.
She wouldn't let her daughter suffer that pain. She
just wouldn't.

Anna looked at her mother, seeming even smaller
now that she was hunched in on herself. The sounds
of familiar tears coming from her shaking body.

Eamon poked his head around the entrance to the
snug. There was pity in his eyes, and she hated him
for it. She hated this whole damn village.

'I'll make sure she's okay for the night.'

'Do that,' Anna said as she walked out of the pub
with her head held high. She wouldn't let them see
her cry. She never had.

Anna didn't notice that the rain had stopped as she

made her way back to the small family business she had barely managed to hold on to through the years. All she could think of was her little daughter, Amalia. Her gorgeous dark brown eyes, and thick curly hair. Sounds of her laughter, her tears and the first cries she'd made on this earth echoed in her mind. And the miraculous moment that, after being placed in her arms for the first time, Amalia opened her eyes and Anna had felt…love. Pure, unconditional, heart-stopping love. There was nothing she wouldn't do for her daughter.

The day she'd discovered that she was pregnant with Dimitri's child was the day that his sentence had been handed to him by the American judge. She'd almost felt the gavel fall onto the bench, as if it had tolled against her own heart. She'd never wanted to believe him guilty of the accusations levelled at him, the theft of millions of dollars from the American clients of the Kyriakou Bank, but what had she known of him then? Only that he was a man who liked whisky, had driven her to the highest of imaginable pleasures and left her bed the following morning without a word.

Hating to think that her child would bear the stigma of such a parent, she'd determined to keep the identity of Amalia's father to herself. But when she'd heard of his innocence? And tried to get in touch with him? Only to hear that she was just one of several women making the same 'claim'? She practically growled at the memory. Her daughter wasn't a claim. Amalia had been eight months old, and from that day she'd promised to be both mother and father to her child. She'd promised to ensure that Amalia would be happy, secure and know above all that she was loved. She wanted to give her daughter the one thing she had never had growing up after her own father had abandoned his pregnant wife.

As she walked up path towards the front of the bed and breakfast she could see a small minibus in the driveway. The three customers who had checked in earlier that day were stowing their bags in the back.

Mr Carter and his wife saw her first.

'This is absolutely unacceptable. I'll be adding this to my review.'

'What's going on?' she demanded, her interruption momentarily stopping Mr Carter's tirade.

'We booked with you in good faith, Ms Moore. I suppose the only good thing is that we're upgrading to the hotel in town. But really. To be kicked out with no explanation at ten thirty at night… Not good, Ms Moore. Not good.'

Before Anna could do anything further, her customers disappeared onto the bus. She jumped out of the way as it backed out of the drive, leaving only one man standing in front of the door to her home.

Dimitri Kyriakou. Looking just as furious as she felt.

Dimitri had been pacing the small bar where he'd first met Mary Moore. Somewhere in the back of the building a member of Mary's staff was holding his daughter in her arms and looking at him as if he were the devil.

From inside, he heard the irate conversation from one of the customers. She'd returned.

In just a few strides Dimitri exited the bar, passed along the short hallway and out through the front door, just in time to see the bus departing.

He'd let anger drive him out here, but he was stopped in his tracks the moment he caught sight of the woman who had nearly, *nearly*, succeeded in separating him from his child.

Tendrils of long, dark hair whipped around her face, her green eyes bright with something he could recognise. Anger was far too insipid a word for the storm that was brewing between them. She looked… incredible. And he hated her for it. She was better than any of his imprisoned dreams could have conjured. But wasn't that how the devil worked? Looking like the ultimate temptation whilst cutting out a soul?

'What are you doing here? And what have you done to my guests?' she demanded.

The hostility in her tone was nothing he'd ever imagined hearing from her lips. But he was happy to hear it. Happy to have it match his own.

'We need to talk; they were in the way. I got rid of them.'

Money was an incredible thing. It had been both his saviour and his destroyer, but this time he was going to use it to help him get what he wanted… what he *needed*.

The woman holding his daughter moved into the hallway behind him, drawing Mary's attention. He watched as the mother of his child rushed past him, forcing him to back out of her way, and swept their daughter up in her arms.

They made a striking image, Mary's dark head buried in the crook of their daughter's neck. He'd so desperately wanted to hold his child the first moment he set eyes on her. But the woman employed by Mary had raged that she wouldn't let her be held by a stranger. *Christe mou*, was this how he started as a father? Being denied the right to hold his child? Anger crushed his chest.

'Thank you, Siobhan. You can go now.'

'If you're sure?' the young girl asked, casting him a doubtful look. After a quick nod of reassurance from the woman holding his child, the girl brushed past him, letting loose a low tut as she did so.

Dimitri locked his gaze with Mary's. If looks could kill...

It was all Anna could do to take him in. Dimitri filled the entire doorway, looking like the devil come to collect his dues. Tall, broad and mouthwatering. Anger slashed his cheeks and made a mockery of the taut bones of his incredible features. The long, dark, handmade woollen coat hung almost to his knees, covering a dark blue knitted jumper that, she knew, would stretch across his broad shoulders perfectly. Broad shoulders that she'd once draped with her hands, her fingers, her tongue. Even the sight

of him drove away the bone-deep chill that had settled into her skin from the rain. Her body's betrayal
stung as it vibrated, coming to life for the first time
in three years, just from his proximity. Desire coated
her throat while heat flayed her skin.

He looked as if he'd just stepped from the pages of
a glossy magazine. And there she was, soaking wet,
an old, hideous luminous-green waterproof jacket
covering ill-fitting jeans and a T-shirt that was probably indecently see-through from the rain. But it was
his eyes, shards of obsidian and hauntingly familiar,
so like the ones she'd seen every single day since her
daughter had been placed in her arms. Though they
had never been filled with such disdain.

'You have five minutes.' His voice was harsh and
more guttural than she remembered. Cursing herself
silently, she forced her brain into gear.

'For what?' Anna asked, thinking that this was an
odd way to start the conversation she'd spent years
agonising over.

'To say goodbye.'

'Goodbye to who?'

'Our daughter.'

CHAPTER TWO

Dear Dimitri,
I didn't mean for it to be like this.

INSTINCTIVELY ANNA CLUTCHED Amalia tightly to her chest.

'I'm not saying goodbye to my daughter!'

'Don't play the put-upon mother now.'

Dimitri had taken a step towards her and Anna took a step back.

'You,' Dimitri continued, 'who only two days ago blackmailed me with news of her. The transfer has been made, but I've come to collect. Because there's no way I'm leaving my daughter in the care of an alcoholic, debt-ridden liar and cheat.'

Anna's head spun. So much so, it took her a moment to realise that he had somehow mistaken her for her mother.

'Wait—'

'I've waited long enough.'

Anna watched, horrified, as another man appeared in the doorway. A man who had 'legal' stamped all

over him. It didn't make a dent in Dimitri's powerful tirade.

'Mary Moore of Dublin, Ireland. Mortgaged up
to the hilt, with three drunk and disorderlies, one
child and no father's name on the birth certificate.
You should have been on the stage,' Dimitri spat, his
anger infusing his words with misplaced righteousness. 'The woman I met that night three years ago
was clearly nothing more than a drunken apparition...
with consequences. That consequence—'

'Don't you *dare* call my child a consequence,'
she hissed at him, struggling not to raise her voice
and disturb Amalia, who was wriggling in discomfort already.

'That consequence is why I am here,' he pressed
on. 'Now that I am aware of her existence, I shall be
taking her with me. If it's money you need, then my
lawyer here will draw up the requisite paperwork
for you to sign guardianship over to me. Though I
wouldn't normally pay twice for something, I will
allow it this time.'

'Pay twice for *something*? You're calling my
daughter "something"?' Anna demanded furiously.

His words provoked her beyond all thought. Blood
pounded in her ears; injustice over his awful accusations sang in her veins; fury at his arrogance, anger
at his belief that she would do just as he asked lit a
flame that bloomed, crackled and burned.

'I am sure that it would be possible, *Mr Kyriakou*,
almost easy for you, even, to have your lawyer draw
up paperwork, to hand over ludicrous amounts of

money, money that would be *yours*, I'm sure, not taken from the clients of the Kyriakou Bank…' she paused for breath, ignoring how his darkened eyes had narrowed infinitesimally, before continuing '…were I Mary Moore.'

His head jerked back as if he had been slapped.

'Mary Moore is guilty of all the things you have lambasted her for. She is the one who contacted you demanding money for her silence. But I. Am. Not. Mary. Moore. I'm *Anna* Moore. And if you raise your voice to me in front of our daughter *one more time*, I'll throw you out myself!'

In her mind she had been shouting, hurling those words against the invisible armour he seemed to wear about him. But in reality she had been too conscious of her daughter, too much of a mother to do anything that would upset her child. But she had caught Dimitri on the back foot—she could see that from the look of shock, then quick calculation as he assessed the new information. And she was determined to press her advantage.

'I will call the police if I have to,' Anna continued. 'And with your record—even expunged—I think you'll find that they'll side with me. At least for tonight.'

The smirk on his cruel lips infuriated her.

'My lawyer would have me out in an hour.'

'The same lawyer that told me he'd pay me off, *"just like the last one"*, when I tried to tell you of our child's birth?'

Dimitri spun round to look at David in confusion.

But David seemed just as confused as he. 'It wasn't me,' his friend said, shaking his head. 'I don't know anything about that.'

'What? When did this happen?' he demanded, already beginning to feel unsteady on the shifting sands beneath his feet.

'When you were first freed from prison nineteen months ago, I called your office. You may like to think that I purposefully kept my daughter from you, but I did try to reach out to you,' Mary—*Anna*—said from over his shoulder. Reluctantly he turned back round to look her in the eye, needing to see the truth of her words. 'He referred to himself as Mr Tsoutsakis. It's not something I'm likely to forget.'

'*Theos*, that was my ex-assistant and, I assure you, he will never work again,' Dimitri swore, still trying to wrap his head around the fact that Anna had tried to reach him for something other than bribery or money.

'I don't care who it was. I was told, in rather specific terms, that I would be paid off, just like the other hundred or so women calling to claim they had carried the heir to the Kyriakou Bank. I had—and still have—no intention of taking money from you, or depriving whatever number of illegitimate children you fathered before, or since, your imprisonment of any child support.'

'There are no other children,' he ground out. 'When I…when I was arrested certain…women sought me out, claiming that I had fathered numerous children unrelated to me.' Their sordid attempts at extortion had snuffed out the last little flame of hope he'd had in human decency. To use a child in such a way was horrific to him. In total four women had jumped on the wrong bandwagon, assuming he'd pay for their silence. But none of them, neither his two ex-girlfriends nor the two strangers who had claimed an acquaintance with him, had realised that he would never, *never* let a child of his disappear from his life. Dimitri resisted the urge to reach out to Anna. 'I swear to you. There were no other women, no other children.'

'And I'm supposed to just believe you?' Her scorn cut him to the quick. 'So, this is your lawyer? Tell me, *Mr Lawyer*, what would the courts say to a man who turns up at ten thirty at night making false accusations of alcoholic behaviour, costing me three bookings and irreconcilable damage to my professional reputation, threatening to take my daughter away from me and trying to blackmail me?'

And, finally, it was then that their daughter started to cry.

'You're making her upset,' Dimitri accused.

'No, *you* are,' she returned.

Feeling the ground beneath him start to slip further, Dimitri pressed on, ignoring his own internal warning bell.

'It's neither here nor there. You need to pack. Get your things—we're leaving,' he commanded. Even to his own ears he sounded obtuse. But he couldn't help it. It was this situation…his childhood memories clawing their way up from the past and into the present making him rash, making him desperate.

'I'm not going anywhere and I really will call the police if you try to force me. You clearly don't know the first thing about parenting if you're expecting it to be okay to just upend a child at ten thirty at night.'

'And whose fault is that?' he heard himself shout, immediately regretting his loss of control. Nothing about this situation had gone as he'd intended and that there was a grain of truth in her last accusation struck him deeply.

David shifted in the hallway, drawing their attention.

'My recommendation is to sleep on this a little. Clearly there has been a series of misunderstandings and we each need time to reflect on the new information we all have. Dimitri, we should take the car back to Dublin and return in the morning.'

'I'm not leaving my daughter,' Dimitri growled.

'Ms Moore, is this something that you are happy to accommodate?'

Dimitri almost couldn't look at her, didn't want to gauge her reaction. When he'd walked into this, he'd been so sure. Sure of his plan, of his information, of the situation. Yet the moment she'd revealed that she wasn't Mary, but Anna, he *knew* she wasn't lying. He'd felt the truth of it settle about his shoulders and, looking at it now, he was relieved. The woman who had given birth to his daughter wasn't an alcoholic. Hadn't been arrested. The woman he'd slept with and spent years dreaming about... Layers and layers of cloudy images began to shift, and when he opened his eyes he looked at Anna and they became clear.

Anna was looking down at her daughter, rocking her gently in her arms as she settled their child, making soothing noises that seemed to satisfy the girl…his daughter. And he held his breath before her pronouncement. He felt, rather than heard, her sigh.

'I'll put him in one of the recently vacated rooms. I'm not comfortable with the way he's done things.' It irked him that she was directing her conversation to David rather than him, but he had to be fair. It was justified after the accusations he'd hurled at her. And Dimitri knew a thing or two about wrongful accusations. 'But we do,' she continued, 'need to talk and figure out where we go from here.'

Dimitri followed David out to the car, assuring David that he wasn't such a monster as to cause harm or fear to his daughter or the mother of his child, especially given that she was clearly not the woman he had thought from the report. He took several deep breaths of cool night air before returning to the small bed and breakfast. Peeking into empty rooms on the ground floor, he felt like a trespasser in his daughter's home and hated it.

He followed the soothing sounds of a gentle lullaby that contrarily only fuelled the anger within him. How many nights had he missed the simple pleasure of putting his daughter to bed, knowing that she was safe, cared for…loved? He paused on the threshold of a dusky-pink room, gently lit by a softly glowing night light.

Dimitri looked at the nearly sleeping child in the crib. She was peaceful and angelic. He knew that was a cliché, but he couldn't think of any other words to describe his daughter. It was the first time he'd really *seen* her, not hidden by the shoulder of a stranger or buried in her mother's arms. Her skin was dark, like both her parents', but the eyes—they were his. He knew that Anna hadn't seen him yet, her body hadn't stiffened the way it had every single time he'd come within a foot of her. But she was far from relaxed, and he deeply regretted that their adult emotions had come to interfere with his child's sleep.

How had this mess happened? She'd been shocked by Dimitri's accusations, his presence…all of it. For nineteen months, she'd forced herself to abandon the hope that he might come for her. The hope that her daughter wouldn't grow up feeling that same sense of rejection that felt almost a solid part of Anna. But that was the thing—Anna's father hadn't just been absent, it wasn't a passive thing…he had walked away. Had actively chosen to leave her and her mother behind.

She pushed at the adrenaline still pounding through her veins, desperately fighting the need to flee. Instead, she clung to the words she'd spoken to the lawyer. They really did need to find a way forward, now that he knew about Amalia, now that he claimed to *want* their child. Wasn't that what she'd dreamed of when she first reached out to him? Never would she have chosen to raise her daughter without a father in her life…the way she had been raised.

As Anna watched her daughter in the crib, she marvelled at how she'd got so big. She was twenty-seven months old and before lying down on the soft mattress Amalia had held on to the bars and looked at Anna with big brown eyes. Anna had reached out and smoothed a soft curl of hair from Amalia's forehead. She'd bent down and whispered a promise to her child.

'It will be okay, sweetheart. It will.' She'd hoped that she wasn't lying.

Anna waited until she heard the sounds of her daughter's breathing slow. She waited until she knew she couldn't put it off any more and turned to leave the room.

But Dimitri stood in the doorway.

How many times had she imagined him standing there? How many times, during Amalia's sleepless nights, the teething, the crying…the times when Anna had been so exhausted she couldn't even weep? What would she have given to see him standing there, a support, a second hand, anything to help take away some of the weight of being a single parent?

But when she'd heard the lawyer—the assistant, as she now knew—dismiss her claims as one of the many women who had called Dimitri, she'd realised that she hadn't known Dimitri at all. The disbelief and incredulity in Tsoutsakis's voice had been the reminder she'd clung to each and every night that she had been right to hang up the phone, to end the conversation before she could reveal any more of herself, of her daughter.

But now? What did it all mean? That it hadn't been Dimitri who had outright rejected his daughter. That he was innocent of the imprisonment that had made her sure she couldn't let a criminal be the father of her child. Now that he was here, standing before her.

'I don't even know her name.' Anna read a whole host of emotions in that one sentence: pain, regret… anger.

'Amalia. Her name is Amalia.'

For a second, he looked as if he had been punched in the chest… He closed his eyes briefly but when they opened he wore a mask.

'She's mine.' It was a statement rather than a question. But for all his seeming arrogant certainty, she could tell that he needed to hear it from her. It was as if he was holding his breath.

For just a moment, Anna considered lying. It would all go away. Dimitri would leave and go back to Greece, or America, or wherever he'd come from. Life could return to normal, she'd continue to manage the bed and breakfast, continue to handle her mother's alcoholism, continue to raise her daughter on her own. But she couldn't do it. She knew what it was like to grow up in this small village without a father, with the stigma of being discarded and unwanted. She knew the questions that were sure to come from her daughter's lips because they had come from her own.

Where's my daddy? Didn't Daddy want me? Did he not love me?

His eyes darkened impossibly as she made him wait for her answer.

'Yes. She's your daughter.'

'How?' he bit out. 'We were careful. Every single time. We were careful.'

It was a question she had asked herself time and time again during her pregnancy. Forcing herself to relive that night, the intimacies they'd shared, trying to find the exact moment that their daughter had been conceived.

'Protection fails sometimes,' she said, echoing the words of the female doctor who had looked at her with pity.

Anna followed him out into the hallway, ensuring Amalia's door stayed open just an inch.

He spun round to face her.

'How could you? How could you keep this from me?'

This was the argument that she'd expected. The one she'd rehearsed in the dead of night when she'd known, somehow, that he *would* return and come to claim his child. This was the reason that she had poured hours and months into writing letters—documenting her thoughts, experiences, feelings from the day Amalia was born. Letters that had never been sent, nor read by the intended recipient, because they had been addressed to the father of her child. And this man? This man she did not know.

'You left my bed and within hours were arrested

for massive financial fraud. How could I subject the precious child I carried to a man I barely knew and who was in prison within months?'

'I was *wrongfully* imprisoned,' he bit out.

'I didn't know that at the time! And the moment I did find out, I was...' She actually growled her frustration. 'You know what I was told.' She tried to take a calming breath. 'Look, let's talk about this in the morning. We both need sleep, or at least I certainly do.' She stopped short of adding 'please' to the sentence. Instinctively she knew that any sign of weakness would be like blood in the water to a shark. She waited, her breath held, until the almost imperceptible nod of his head signalled his agreement.

Anna led Dimitri down the hallway to a room. Admittedly it was the smallest room she had to offer, but right now Anna was going to take any small victory she could. Did it make her petty? Perhaps. But she was too tired to care.

Only she hadn't been prepared for the sight of his large build in the small room. She hadn't braced herself for the memories that rushed to greet her of the last time he'd spent the night under this roof.

He'd swept into her life when she had been at her lowest, when she had felt helpless against the failings of *both* her parents. When all she'd wanted was something for herself. Just for once. One night that wasn't about being responsible or putting someone else's needs above her own.

She'd told herself that she would stop at one drink. She'd told herself she'd stop at one kiss, one touch...

and after he'd given her pleasure she had never imagined possible she'd told herself she only wanted one
night. But that had been a lie.

Until she'd woken, alone. The dull ache that took
up residence in her heart that morning robbed her
of the pleasure and the reckless need for one stolen
night. In that moment she was cured of any selfish
want she'd ever have, and she'd promised never to
lose herself like that again. But she had never regretted that night. And she never would. For it had
brought her Amalia.

Dimitri looked around the small room. It was little bigger than the cell he'd had in prison, but the
exhaustion in Anna's eyes had struck a nerve. He'd
come here, all guns blazing, expecting to sweep in
and take his child away from a mother who couldn't
care less about his child. What he'd seen instead was
a beautiful woman who was fiercely protective of her
child. A woman who had raised a child alone, just as
his own mother once had. Perhaps he should take the
time to work this new information into his plans, before trying again. As if sensing his resolution, Anna
backed out quietly from the small room, and Dimitri
sat heavily on the surprisingly comfortable mattress.

David was probably helping himself to a whisky
from the hotel's minibar right now, Dimitri thought as
he pulled off his shoes. But he wouldn't have changed
places with the man. He was sleeping less than twenty
metres from his daughter. From his own child. And
he knew that he'd never let her out of his sight again.

* * *

A loud crashing sound from below jerked Dimitri from the fitful sleep he'd fallen into. Terror raced through his bones for just a second, until he saw the faint outline of flowery wallpaper and felt the soft mattress beneath him. He wasn't back in prison. No one was about to get hurt. He waited for a moment to get his breath back, for the painful sting of adrenaline to recede from his pores.

But then the crash sounded again, and his daughter started to cry. *What the hell?*

He launched out of the bed and into the hallway, where he met Anna.

'Anna, what—?'

'Go back to bed,' she whispered harshly. 'Please, just—'

Another crashing sound came, this time accompanied by the sound of breaking glass.

He caught a look of panic passing across Anna's features before she disappeared down the stairs. Amalia was starting to cry in earnest now, and he went into her room. Did he pick her up? Would that make her stop, or cry even harder?

Her poor little face was already red, with big, fat tears rolling down her cheeks. The ear-piercing screams of his daughter caught in his heart and he reached down and picked her up, ignoring the stab of hurt as she tried to pull away from him, her strength surprising him.

He held her against his chest and followed Anna's footsteps down to the hallway and the bar below, thinking he was ready for whatever he would find down there. But he wasn't.

Anna was on the floor, kneeling before a small red-haired woman, who was trying to shake Anna off.

'Please, Ma. You need to go.'

'You left me with that man—'

'You know Eamon, Ma.'

Dimitri watched as Anna's mother tried to get out of the chair, pushing Anna away and nearly succeeding, until Anna stood and took her by the shoulders.

'Ma, please. It's late and you've woken Amalia.'

For a moment, that seemed to do the trick. 'My precious Amalia…' But the moment she caught sight of Dimitri standing with her granddaughter, any hold that Anna might have had on her mother disappeared.

She knocked Anna off balance and she fell awkwardly on her knee. Mary took two uncertain steps towards him and Dimitri instinctively turned to protect his daughter, angling his body away from the drunk woman. He held out his arm.

'Enough!' His strong command brought the older woman to a standstill. 'Anna, take Amalia upstairs.'

Anna looked for a moment as if she was about to argue, but clearly thought better of it.

She took her daughter from him, their skin brushing against each other's for the first time since that night three years before. Ignoring the waves of little pinpricks that rushed over his hands, Dimitri watched as Anna disappeared up the stairs, her last glance at them uncertain and worried.

Dimitri stared at the woman in front of him, seeing very little trace of Anna's colouring, but for just a moment he could see reflections of what must have once made the older woman beautiful, especially in the startling moss-green eyes looking back at him.

Dimitri wasn't a stranger to what alcohol could do to a person and what kind of chemical prison it could be. Some responded to gentle persuasion, but the time for that had passed.

'I'm going to get you some water, and you're going to sleep down here on the sofa.' There was no way he was going to let her upstairs near his child or her daughter. Mary made one last effort to complain, but he saw that off with a raised eyebrow.

'Do not test me, Mrs Moore. You've done enough damage tonight.'

She just hadn't realised how much yet.

As Mary reluctantly lay down on the sofa, Anna stuck her head over the bannisters. He raised a hand to stop her from coming further down the stairs, knowing that her reappearance would spark another round from the woman on the sofa.

Anna's eyes were sad as she mouthed the words 'thank you' to him and disappeared. And just for a moment he felt sorry for her. Because she had no idea what was about to happen.

He waited until Mary Moore fell into a comfortably drunk sleep and pulled out his mobile. David answered on the second ring.

'I need you to do a couple of things for me. I need indefinite management cover for the bed and breakfast and a list of rehab clinics as far away from this village as humanly possible, and I need both by ten a.m. tomorrow.'

'Sure thing. Anything else?'

'Yes. Tell Flora to get the house prepared for anything a two-year-old might need. And after that, I want you to start working on a watertight prenup.'

CHAPTER THREE

Dear Dimitri,
How could you do such a thing?

ANNA FLIPPED OUT the bed sheet, the whipping sound it made before it settled over the mattress making her wince. She was exhausted, having barely slept the night before. Every time she'd closed her eyes she'd seen Dimitri standing between her and Amalia as if it were a prophecy foretelling how she would, from now on, see her daughter—at a distance and with him separating them. If not that, then she'd been tortured by the memories of her own pleasure as Dimitri had teased orgasm after orgasm from her innocent body.

But when she woke, all she could think of was her mother. It had been years since Mary had turned up at the bed and breakfast that far out of control. A twinge cramped her stomach. This hadn't been the life she'd wanted. Once she'd dreamed of escaping the small village, whose inhabitants had been hostile towards them from the moment Mary had been forced to raise her child alone. Anna had fantasised about studying art and sculpture, perhaps even at the University of Glasgow. It had been a hope that she'd cherished as she'd worked at the bed and breakfast saving every penny she made to put towards tuition fees. That Anna had somehow managed to follow in her mother's footsteps—becoming, instead, another single mother—had sealed their fate. Undesirable. Unwanted. The cautionary tale that locals told their children. And what a cautionary tale it was. Only the masochistic would want Dimitri Kyriakou arriving on their doorstep to claim what he felt he was owed.

By the time the sun had peeked around her curtain that morning, she'd realised she needed a plan. She needed to take back the control that was slipping through her fingers like hot sand.

This was the last of the rooms that needed cleaning after the hasty departure of her guests the night before. If she was lucky, she'd be able to pull some new clients from the horse racing meeting in Dublin in a few days' time.

Thankfully her mother had left before Anna had brought Amalia down for breakfast. It was the one showdown she hadn't been prepared for. Where her mother was concerned, Anna realised that she no longer had any defences left. How could her mother have done that, knowing Amalia was in the house? Clearly all the talk of rehab—the apparent reason she'd taken the money from Dimitri in the first place—was a… Anna wasn't ready to call it a lie, more of a thin spider's web of fiction that broke under the weight of addiction.

Rehab had been a mythical promise she'd heard over and over again throughout the years. A place the woman wearing her mother's skin would go, and upon her return would be her real mother gifted back to her. The mother who had once been a bright, powerful, creative woman with a deep well of love to give and not enough pools in which to store it. But her mother was one problem. Dimitri was another.

There were a hundred different ways she'd imagined their reunion, and not one of them came remotely close to what had happened the night before. Recalling the night they'd spent together three years before, she realised that she'd been wearing her mother's shirt—the one with the name Mary Moore sewn onto the pocket. And, with her mother's record, would *she* not have stormed in like a Valkyrie, ready to retrieve her child from such a woman? The way that no one had done for her?

She felt, rather than heard, a presence behind her. Siobhan was downstairs with Amalia, so there was only one person it could be. Only one person had ever had that effect on her body. It had been the same way the first time she'd laid eyes on him. A feeling that the world had ever so slightly tilted on its axis, a feeling that nothing would ever be the same again. It started on her forearms, as if she were held there between powerful hands, raising the hairs beneath the imaginary touch. It licked up her spine and across her neck. And then Anna cursed herself for being fanciful.

'What are you doing?' Dimitri asked, sounding as sleep-deprived as she.

'Preparing the rooms. I may get some walk-ins later. The weather is good, and the races are on...' She trailed off, knowing that she had to address what had happened with her mother. 'About last night—'

'Does she live here?'

'My mother? No.' Anna shook her head vehemently, instantly understanding his concern. 'No. It's been years since she turned up here like that.'

'Who else do you employ here?' It wasn't perhaps the question she'd expected. She'd imagined Dimitri would haul her over the coals for her mother's appearance. Anna was still trying to gather her thoughts from the breakneck speed of his inquisition. She still hadn't turned to face him. She needed just a moment more to gather her strength.

'Siobhan helps out when we're at capacity. Which we would have been today, had not all my customers been removed to a hotel in Dublin.' With this she finally turned to take in the broad expanse of the man who had no damn right to look that good after a night in the smallest room she had.

Instantly regretting it, she turned back to the room, picked up the cleaning basket and made her way into the en suite bathroom. She put on the rubber gloves and spread a healthy squirt of bleach on the scrubber as if she could clean away either the sight of him or him completely.

She got onto her knees, realising that this was perhaps the most ridiculous way to have a conversation, but, needing something to do with her hands other than throttle the man behind her, she pushed on.

'I've been thinking, and I would like you to have a relationship with my—*our*—daughter.' She told herself it was the smell of the bleach that had her stomach twisting and turning worse than any morning sickness she had experienced. 'I'd be happy to grant visitation rights, but you must understand that we will be staying here. My life is here and so is my daughter's. I will not uproot everything she's ever known.'

There. She had managed to get the words from her mind to her mouth without crying, or sounding weak. She needed him to agree to this.

For a moment, just as he had done the night before, he felt almost sorry for her. She had no idea that her life was about to change irrevocably. But from the first time he'd heard of his daughter, Dimitri knew that he wouldn't settle for visitation rights. He wanted his daughter with him. All the time.

He was man enough to admit that the knowledge that he currently didn't have any legal rights to his child was nothing short of terrifying. The fear that had gripped him in those first moments of this shocking discovery had been nothing like anything he'd ever experienced. *Nothing.* Even when he'd arrived at his father's house at the age of seven for the first time, not knowing if he'd take him in. Even before that, when the police filling the tiny apartment he'd shared with his mother were saying unintelligible things that he struggled to make sense of years after they had left his life. None of it scratched the surface of the deep well that opened up when he realised that there was a tiny life out there, his flesh and blood...

'I don't want you to miss out on things,' Anna was saying as she furiously scrubbed at the toilet, before picking herself up off the floor and turning—still with her back to him—to the sink.

'You don't want me missing...' His sentence trailed off as incredulity hit him hard. 'What, like the first sonogram? The first sound of my daughter's heartbeat? Tell me, Anna,' he said, reaching out to pull her around to him, so that he could look her in the eyes, so he could see the truth written there in them when she answered his next question. 'Does my daughter even know the word *Daddy*?'

He regretted touching her the moment his fingers hit the bare skin of her arm beneath her short T-shirt. He tried to ignore the flames that licked out at him from just one touch; he tried to ignore the rush of memories he'd held at bay for the last two days. He had to. Instead, he focused on the mounting horror in Anna's eyes.

'What? Did you think I wouldn't have wanted to be part of those things? *Christe mou*, Anna, did you even think of me at all?'

Dimitri cursed again, but this time silently. He hadn't want to reveal that much. He needed to get this back on to an unemotional level if he had any hope of persuading her to his cause. But the more and more he thought of all the things he had missed out on, all of the things Amalia would have grown up with, the stigma of being illegitimate in a sternly familial culture…and at how he hadn't been able to protect her from that… He knew how much damage could be done to a child when they were unwelcome, unwanted…

So, no. No. He'd never put his daughter through that. He would do what he had to do. Because that was what Dimitri did. He put aside anything that would prevent the required outcome. He cut off the thoughts of the past, his mother, his half-brother's betrayal, thoughts of the time he had spent wrongfully incarcerated in prison. They had no place here. Here was his daughter. And the mother of his child. And he needed them in Greece.

'This is getting us nowhere,' he said, looking around the small bathroom. 'Can we… Do you have coffee? Can we sit and have a proper conversation, when you're not…?' He gestured towards the cleaning products and the hideous yellow gloves Anna was wearing.

The smell of coffee seemed to have a calming effect on his nerves, but the moment the insipid, thin liquid hit his tongue he regretted it. Dimitri kept his eyes trained on Anna, who had yet to stop moving,

either around the small bathroom she'd been cleaning or the impressive, sleek chrome kitchen he'd been
surprised to find tucked away from the main part of
the old cottage.

He supposed the small staff area could pass as
cosy and compact. But while he sat pressed up
against the wall, his long legs barely fitting beneath
the wooden table, his patience finally wore thin.

'Sit down,' he demanded.

Anna stilled, freezing against the command, but
finally she slipped—easily—into the seat opposite
him. Though her body had finally stopped moving,
her eyes seemed to take everything in but him.

'I want you to come to Greece.'

Ah. That did it. Anna's gaze zeroed in on his.

'No.'

'No?' he asked, his eyebrow raised.

She let out an incredulous laugh. 'How can I go
to Greece? I have a business here, my mother, my…
life is here, Dimitri. I can't.'

This was nothing he hadn't expected, but the
email he'd received from David that morning had
confirmed that everything was in place. In fact, in
just five short minutes Anna would see how point-
less her arguments would be. He didn't want to use
her mother's behaviour from the night before against
her. But even if Mary didn't live under the same roof
she was still an influence on his daughter's life, she
could still put his daughter at risk. So he *would* use
it if Anna forced him to. First he'd try a softer approach. And if that didn't work…

'Anna. The situation you're in can't be easy. The bank is about to take all this away from you.' He ignored the small gasp of shock that fell from her mouth.

'How do you—?'

'And between Amalia and your mother, dealing with all that alone—'

'I haven't been alone—'

'—must have been incredibly trying. All the work that you have to do here… You must be exhausted. It certainly can't allow you the time you'd like to dedicate to our daughter.' That there was no interruption this time told him all he needed to know. 'I want to pay off the mortgage—in your name. I will also pay for your mother to go to a rehab clinic. Anna, your mother needs help. Proper help. And I can provide that.

'A lovely couple is ready and willing to run the bed and breakfast in your absence, just for a short time, whilst you come to Greece. There, Amalia can get to know me, get to know her Greek heritage, her family.' Forestalling her objections, he pressed on. 'Anna, it's something that you deserve—time away from this place, to relax and to spend time with your daughter without having to worry about keeping the roof together over your heads.'

Anna's head spun. In her wildest dreams she had wanted this. She had wanted someone to sweep in, take care of everything, to resolve all her financial worries, to help with her mother, to allow her to focus solely on her daughter. In her deepest heart,

she'd even wanted that person to be Dimitri. Like
the fairy-tale prince and the happy-ever-after that
she had never thought was possible. But, just like
in all good fairy tales, Dimitri's offer was surely
too good to be true. Like the poisoned apple, or the
spindle needle's prick, there was always a price to
pay. And, just like the miller's daughter, there was
no way she would hand over her child.

But for a moment Dimitri's eyes had softened, and
she'd seen glimpses of the man she'd met that night
three years before. The man she'd written secret letters to in the dead of night. The man who three years
ago had looked at her as if she was the one thing that
could save him. And that night, she'd felt the same of
him. That night, she'd needed him. Was it possible
that she needed him now too?

'I also want to apologise,' he pressed on. 'Last
night, I thought the worst. It was a combination of
shock to discover that I was a father, and fear of just
how much I had missed. Anna,' he said, reaching
out to take her hand in his, the rough, tanned skin
caressing hers with surprising softness, 'please, give
me the chance to make up for my actions. I want
the chance to make things right, to get to know my
daughter—to get to know Amalia.'

Of all the things he'd said, it was *this* that truly
undid Anna. The small crack in her heart that had
appeared the day she'd held her daughter in her arms,
alone in the hospital room without anyone to share
that moment with, opened just a little wider. Be-

cause it was the one thing that her father had never wanted of her.

Could she do it? Could she hand over everything to Dimitri and just walk away? Years of having to be the responsible one, having to make the decisions and do what needed to be done, cried, begged and pleaded for her to say *yes*. But the sensible part of her, the cautionary part of her, feared that it would come at too high a price.

Anna thought of her mother. Of how she had been the night before. Of how many times Mary had promised, sobbed and agonised over her own demons. Anna could never afford to send her mother to a rehab clinic—certainly not the kind that Dimitri's money could afford. If it had just been about her and Amalia, perhaps she might have found the strength to say no. But she knew that she'd never forgive herself for not allowing her mother one more chance.

'How long would it be for?' Anna asked, hating the sound of hope in her own voice.

'Not long. A week; two if needed.' If she thought it odd that he hadn't met her eyes as he spoke, it was buried beneath a layer of hope, and a feeling of exhaustion so deep that she clung to his offer like a drowning man clung to the shore.

And when she said yes she ignored the little voice in her head that told her that she'd just signed her life away.

The next few days passed in a blur. Anna had met with the couple that David—Dimitri's lawyer—had found. They seemed kind and were understanding of the situation. They'd had a small hotel themselves but had passed it on to the next generation in their family and were now travelling around Ireland. Anna, to her surprise, liked them. She'd imagined she would feel resentful, but their care and passion for her own business eased the way considerably.

Dimitri had arranged for a car to take Anna and Mary to the rehabilitation clinic. And, once again, Anna had felt that odd sense of surprise. Through the four-hour journey her mind had built up images of a cold, locked-down concrete facility, but instead she discovered a place that rivalled some of the most expensive hotels in Dublin. Being reunited with her mother after that fateful night had seen her mother spiral into the guilty cycle that Anna was familiar with. But there was something else in her mother's eyes now—hope. A hope that Anna tried so hard not to nourish in her breast, but the air of change was upon them and it was contagious.

The clinician they met at the entrance explained that she and Mary were not to have contact for at least a month. Explained why and how this helped with Mary's recovery process and that it was vital for Mary to have the time to focus on herself. Anna would be allowed to call the centre to find out how her mother was doing and was assured that Mary would be in very good hands. Her mother hadn't even looked back as she passed through the glorious white doors to the centre.

And, now that David had appeared with Ama-

lia's and her passports—hers had expired since she'd
last used it—Dimitri had gone out. It was strange,
because Anna had almost become used to his presence, even if he felt like a jailer. The weight of his
constant gaze, as if he couldn't allow her out of his
sight for more than five minutes, had been a pressure
she hadn't realised was there. So instead of Dimitri,
David sat with her in the small staff area, talking
through the process and getting her to sign financial
documents to do with the bed and breakfast. And
once again she pushed down the inner voice that
warned her she was handing over complete control
of her life to Dimitri Kyriakou.

Dimitri hadn't even made it two miles from the B & B
before he'd pulled over on a quiet country road. He
was supposed to be in Dublin at the race series for
the second leg of the Hanley Cup; he was supposed
to be with the two other members of the Winners'
Circle, Antonio and Danyl—men who were more
family to him than any blood relation could ever
be. But the invisible thread tying him to his child,
to Anna...it didn't stretch that far yet. If Anna knew,
or even suspected, what was about to happen, she'd
run and take his daughter with her. He just couldn't
take the risk.

Tomorrow they would be on his private jet and
once they were in Greece, once they landed on *his*
soil, the power would be all his. But tonight? Tonight, though he couldn't be there in body, there was

no way in hell that he would miss the second race in the Hanley Cup.

He stared at the screen of his tablet, blocking out the sounds of the driving rain, casting the outside world in a blur.

He watched the build-up to the race live, glad that the storm hadn't yet reached Dublin. Nineteen months ago, just after his release, the Australian female jockey Mason McAulty had approached them in a London hotel with such an outrageous proposal it had momentarily silenced all three members of the Winners' Circle. She'd promised to win each of the three legs of the Hanley Cup riding one of their syndicate's horses; a feat which hadn't been achieved in twenty years.

As the camera panned up to the viewing box reserved for the Winners' Circle, Dimitri caught sight of Antonio's brooding Italian face, the grim set to his lips only softening when Emma Guilham—his PA turned fake fiancée, turned very much *real* fiancée—stepped up beside him. Dimitri had often wondered what might have happened had he not been able to convince Antonio to step back from his path to revenge and embrace the one that led him to Emma. Dimitri realised with a start that counselling his friend had been oddly prophetic. He'd certainly not imagined himself to ever consider matrimony. He'd never thought he'd need to.

The high-pitched siren sound of the race starting called his attention back to the horses on the screen.

McAulty was riding a new horse from their syndicate, Devil's Advocate, a gorgeous dark brown thoroughbred. Horse and rider seemed as one as they fluidly spun round the sweeps and curves of the course.

The familiar taste of adrenaline hit the back of his throat, his heart racing as if it were he on the horse and not Mason. After a strong start she'd been pushed back into third place, but she was passing her competitor, quickly checking behind her, urging Devil's Advocate on and gaining on the second.

Dimitri, his heart in his mouth, watched from nearly seventy miles away as they rounded the last bend and looked towards the stretch of flat before the finish line. Mason was still in second place... And then, incredibly, he saw her flash the briefest of smiles and a burst of speed exploded from Devil's Advocate, at first inching his way to pass the lead horse then leaping ahead to a thundering victory.

The noise from the tablet was deafening. His phone started ringing in his pocket and as the camera panned to Antonio and Danyl in the box he saw Danyl turning away with a phone pressed against his ear.

'Did you see? We won!' his friend exclaimed the moment that Dimitri answered.

'Yes, it was a great race,' replied Dimitri, his voice controlled and belying the momentary pleasure coursing through his veins.

'Where are you?'

'Dealing with something.'

'Something? That sounds intriguing even for you, my friend.'

'It's nothing I can't handle on my own,' he said, hoping to God that he was right.

'You know we'd help. Anything.'

Dimitri felt a smile grace his lips. 'I know you'd try to move mountains, Sheikh, and think yourself capable of it, but...'

'You only need ask, Dimitri.'

'Actually there is something. I'd like you and Antonio to come to Greece.'

'You know we wouldn't miss the charity gala—'

'It's not that. It's...for my wedding.' It was the first time that Dimitri had said it out loud. He might not have told Anna yet, nor got her agreement, but he would on both counts. He didn't miss the shocked silence from the other end of the phone. And it took a lot to shock this sheikh.

'Of course we will come. When?'

'Soon. The moment I know, you'll know.'

'Does she have a name?'

'Anna. It's...complicated.'

'You once said nothing would cause you to take a wife, unless...'

Dimitri cursed his friend's quick mind.

'It happened just before I was arrested. My daughter, Amalia, she's twenty-seven months and—' he couldn't prevent the sigh from escaping his lips '—she's incredible.' For the first time, the first real time, he let it sink through his skin, into his bones, deep: he was a father.

'Congratulations, Dimitri,' his closest friend replied, the sincerity in his tone soothing some of the fears he'd had about sharing the news of his new-found family. 'I cannot wait to meet them.'

He nodded, unable to shift the thanks from his mind to his mouth, instead changing the subject. 'How's Mason doing?'

There was a barely perceptible pause before his friend replied, 'She's fine. She's planning to return to Sydney tomorrow.'

'Already? I don't think she's even left the back of the horse yet,' Dimitri said, scanning his tablet for the current footage of the racecourse.

'She's…quite determined.'

Dimitri let out a huff of air, thinking that the description could equally be applied to Anna.

'Good luck with that,' he said to Danyl as much as himself.

'Why would I need luck? Mason is nothing to me, other than our jockey.'

Dimitri wasn't so sure of that and signed off not too long later. He switched off his tablet and listened for a moment to the pounding of the rain, wondering how it was that he could still hear his own heartbeat ringing in his ears. In just a few more hours, Anna and Amalia would be on Greek soil. And then he'd have everything he'd need.

It was late by the time they eventually arrived at Dimitri's island home just off the coast of main-land Greece. Anna had spent the last hour put-ting a fractious, overly excited Amalia to bed and walked through the adjoining door into the considerably larger room that was to be hers. Was this what Dimitri's life was like? In Ireland one day, Greece the next?

Was it normal to feel so disorientated—so nauseous—from even such a short flight? Or was it the fact that she'd handed over the keys to her business, her security, her life to strangers and followed the father of her child to Europe?

She hadn't been prepared for the pack of paparazzi awaiting the arrival of the private jet. Oh, Dimitri had warned her of it; she just hadn't taken him seriously. Closing her eyes now, she could still see the strobe of flashbulbs in the dark. If she listened hard she could still hear the rapid-fire questions, most in Greek, but a surprising few in English.

'Is it true that you carried the heir to the Kyriakou Bank?'

'Is that the child?'

'Where have you been all these years?'

'Why did you hide...?'

Ignoring the swell of emotions in her chest, Anna focused on how her body still vibrated from the boat trip from Piraeus, the boat that Dimitri had piloted himself, standing tall and proud at the wheel, as if he were a marauding pirate rather than an international tycoon—an image that had fired her fevered imagination and brought too many memories of that night from three years ago to the surface.

The powerful speedboat thrilled Amalia as it crested waves and cut through the water as if it were air, but it had only made Anna's heart sink further. Who had the money for such a boat? But then she had seen the house Dimitri had brought her to...

The large, low-hung moon picked out sleek, modern lines that winked at her in the night, hinting at a luxury that felt surreal. She'd glimpsed an infinity pool beyond a patio that opened out to the elements, partitioned off by a plastic rail with a gate—clearly a new addition, since it stood out like a sore thumb. While it touched her that Dimitri had thought of Amalia's safety, she wondered if perhaps that was how *she* seemed, painfully and obviously out of place.

Questions burst through her mind as she wondered if she had denied her daughter by not trying hard enough to tell Dimitri about their child. When they entered his house, toys fit for a princess, still in their boxes, littered the living room and guilt swirled in her stomach. What would Amalia's life have been like if she'd had this from birth? Rather than working all hours in the day, could she have given Amalia finer clothes, better toys and, more importantly, more of herself? She'd done the best she could, she told herself sternly.

'I came to see how you were settling in.'

She closed her eyes against Dimitri's intrusion. Yes, that had been what she'd told him before disappearing into the room she had been given. But explaining that she just needed some space, from him, from his presence, seemed too much like weakness.

'My things have been put away.'

'I have people to do that.'

Yes, thought Anna. *I was one of those people until a few days ago.* But now? It was only for a few days, she told herself. Amalia would get to spend time with her father, and then she and Amalia would return to the bed and breakfast. So she'd better not get used to this. Because he had an island, and she had a bed and breakfast…because she still was *one of those people.*

'Flora?' she asked.

'Yes.'

Anna had instantly liked Dimitri's housekeeper and could tell the older woman was kind, generous and loving.

She opened her eyes, because not being able to see him only made it worse. His smell, unique and distinctly male, assaulted her senses. From the first moment she'd laid eyes on him, she'd known that she was in trouble. It was as if her body, her soul, had immediately identified him as her undoing. But she wasn't here for him, or for her. She was here for Amalia, so that her daughter could get to know her father. Nothing more.

'Thank you,' she said. Finally breaking the silence that had almost become too much.

'What for?' Dimitri sounded genuinely surprised.

'For everything?' she said, shrugging her shoulders and finally turning to take him in. He'd changed out of his cold-weather clothes, and her heart stopped. Even more devastating, he stood there in dark blue linen trousers that moulded his powerful legs and hugged his lean hips. A light blue shirt, rolled back at the sleeves, revealed firm, tanned forearms and Anna forced herself not to bite her lip.

Her fingers itching to reach out, she searched for a distraction instead. She picked up the small clay sculpture she'd wanted to take to Amalia. Even as a small baby, when the palm-sized sculpture had seemed twice as large in her little hands, Amalia had loved to hold it, grip it, even try to gnaw on it. Throughout it all, the little glazed clay piece had never broken.

She turned it in her hands, rubbing the smooth line of the larger oval shape entwined with a smaller one. She had made it years ago, and she'd never shaken the feeling that the piece had been oddly prophetic: mother and child, cast, glazed and fired long before she'd met Dimitri and started out on this path alone. Or perhaps it had reflected her and her own mother—in a maternal embrace she had long forgotten.

Dimitri frowned, noticing her busy hands.

'What's that?'

'Oh…nothing…it's…' Anna let out a huff of gentle laughter. She shrugged and held it out to him.

When he took it into his large hands, it looked dwarfed by them. She saw him studying it, turning it in his hands, relishing the feel of the smooth tempered blue glaze around the edges.

'It's beautiful,' he said simply and she felt the truth of his words to her soul.

'Thank you,' she replied, trying to press down

the surprising shock of sentiment that rose from the simple compliment.

He paused and she was intrigued as she watched the play of emotions crossing his dark features as he realised what she meant.

'You made this?'

'Yes. Just after finishing school. I'd hoped to... I wanted to go university to study art and sculpture, but...' She trailed off. Her mother, him, her daughter, the bed and breakfast...

Rather than filling the silence, Dimitri just stared at the sculpture in his hands, his thumb working over the edges of the two strangely comforting shapes. He pressed it back into her hands, and Anna was confused by the frown still marking his brow. He was hovering...and she didn't quite know why.

'Do you have our passports?' she asked. Anything to fill the strange, awkward silence. 'I wasn't given them back when we landed.'

Something dark passed over Dimitri's features, and the sick feeling that Anna had been trying to ignore rose fully in her chest.

'I have them.'

'I'd like them back.'

'I'm afraid that's not possible.'

'What do you mean?' Anna asked, her heart in her mouth.

'I'm not giving them back to you.'

'But—'

'No buts. You are now in the position that I was in only a few hours ago. You are on Greek soil, and

Amalia is my child.' His eyes darkened, and the atmosphere between them became heavy with tension. 'You cannot be trusted to raise my daughter in a safe environment. Your mother proved that quite successfully that first night. If you want any kind of rights over your child, if you wish to take her back to Ireland, then you will have to marry me.'

'Marry you?' Anna sputtered as she tried to comprehend what he was saying. 'Marry you? Why would I...?' Shock was short and sharp in her mind. Fear sliced through her like a knife. He thought she couldn't be trusted to take care of her child? All she had *ever* done was take care of Amalia. Everything, she'd done everything, sacrificed everything for her. And her mother...? Betrayal thick and fast spread through her. All her instincts were to take her daughter and run. But where to? And who would help her? She was on an island in a country she didn't speak the language of, and where she knew literally no one. How had she been so stupid? How had she allowed herself to trust this man? This man who, right now, she didn't even recognise.

Dimitri could see the fear in her eyes. He knew what it was like to feel trapped and helpless. But he couldn't allow himself to feel sorry. Not for a minute.

'I'm not reneging on my offer. I will take care of your mother, and your business, should your mother ever want to return and continue to run it. But for now you will agree to marry me, giving me legal rights over my child. I will accept nothing less. And you will not get your passports back until you do.'

'Get out!' she shouted. 'Just get out.'

CHAPTER FOUR

Dear Dimitri,
Will you ever trust me?

ANNA DIDN'T KNOW how she'd slept the night before, unless it was some kind of biological form of self-preservation. She opened her eyes to strange surroundings. Light filtered through the floor-to-ceiling windows that offered the most incredible view of sea and sky. Her head hurt and her mouth was dry. Water. She needed water. She looked over at the side table beside the bed and caught sight of the clock.

Ten thirty a.m.? Shock crashed through her, propelling her up from the bed. She slipped on the sheets and tumbled off the mattress onto the floor. Where was Amalia? Why hadn't she heard her daughter? She was in the room next door and would have heard her, *should* have heard her by now.

She ran to her daughter's room, but it was empty. Had he taken her? Had he left her in this house on her own on the island? His threats from the day before rang in her ears as she headed for the stairs that led to the ground floor.

Her bare feet slapped the cold marble floor and, as she took the stairs two at a time, she slipped and lost her breath. Her feet struck air, gravity pulling her down so hard and so fast she had no time to prepare for the biting pain that struck her leg and back. Her teeth snapped together, cutting into the soft flesh of her tongue. She thrust out her hand to try to break her fall as bone met marble and distantly she was surprised not to hear a crack.

Shouts and cries came from somewhere else in the house and when Anna opened her eyes she saw the horrified look on Flora's face, her arms reaching towards her. Arms that Anna batted away, unthinkingly, blind to all but the only face that she needed to see. Her daughter's.

She tried to stand from where she had fallen, her shaking legs barely holding her up. She reached out to the wall to try and hold herself up but couldn't understand why it kept moving further and further away.

'*Theos mou*, Anna!'

'She wasn't in her room,' she managed to get out.

'Anna, you need to sit down. Are you okay?'

She pushed past Dimitri and painfully made her way to the table where Amalia was sitting in a high chair, now red-faced and howling. Anna poured herself into a seat and her heart finally settled as she put her hand on her daughter's arm, as she could feel her daughter, could see that, although upset, her daughter was there and was okay.

Only then did the hurt and pain of her own body start to come into focus.

'I… I didn't know what you'd done with her, where she was…' Anna started shaking now, whether with fear for her child or shock from the fall she didn't know.

Dimitri had come to the table, watching her, and he was saying something that Anna couldn't quite hear.

'…okay? Are you okay?' he demanded. He'd crouched down in front of the chair, bringing him eye level with her, looking at her as if he expected something from her, and Anna resolutely ignored the concern in his eyes.

'Okay? Seriously?' An avalanche of adrenaline hit her. There were too many emotions crashing through her body to distinguish—fury, anger, shock, pain, fear. 'You don't do that! Ever! You never do that to a woman who has spent the last two years raising a child on her own. What the hell were you thinking?'

Dimitri stood there and she hated him. She weakly struck out at his chest. As her voice became louder and louder Amalia started to cry harder and harder.

'After the stunt you pulled last night…' Anna trailed off.

Dimitri turned and said something to the housekeeper, who was looking at Dimitri as if he were the devil. Flora's furious stream of Greek made Anna feel just a little bit better.

'I'm going to call the doctor,' Dimitri announced, reaching out to help her as she picked up Amalia, clearly worried that she wouldn't be strong enough. One look from Anna stopped his hand mid-air. Anna pulled her daughter onto her lap and hugged her fiercely. He had no idea how strong she could be for her daughter.

'I'm fine. I don't need a doctor.'

His pulse hadn't even begun to settle yet. When he'd seen Anna fall everything had stopped. Including his heart. It must have hurt, and it would be a miracle if she'd not broken a bone. His daughter's crying was just beginning to subside and as he looked Anna over he could see a nasty grazed bruise beginning to appear on her calf. Across her slim arms, similar red, angry welts painted her skin and guilt clenched his stomach so tight, worse than anything he'd ever experienced.

Flora came back into the room and gave him a look that could have stopped Hades in his tracks. She placed two bags of frozen vegetables on the table beside Anna, waited for Anna to meet her gaze and cocked her head in the universal body language of *are you okay?* When Anna finally replied in the affirmative, Flora nodded to herself once, rubbed Anna on the arm gently and held her hands out to take the now silent Amalia.

Dimitri watched, fascinated, as Anna handed over their daughter to his housekeeper in a way she'd never done with him. Flora took Amalia out into the garden, making sure to stay where they could both be seen by Anna.

Shame and guilt hit him hard. He'd wanted to spend some time with his daughter. He'd even wanted Anna to get some proper rest. He knew what she'd been through in the last few days, what *he'd* put her through. And look what had happened. He wanted to pace, he wanted to run, do something with all the feelings that were coursing through his body in that moment. But he didn't. Because Anna was at the table, and most likely in considerable pain. Frozen peas weren't good enough. He needed to call a doctor.

'I'm truly sorry,' he said, taking the seat next to her, still fearful that she might break into a thousand pieces.

'I don't know you,' she said as if she were talking to a stranger. 'We spent one night together nearly three years ago, and after that? You show up out of nowhere, threaten me, bring me to Greece and are presently engaged in forcing me to marry you. What did you expect me to think when I woke to find my daughter gone?'

'I…' Dimitri was struggling to find the words. Words that would somehow make her understand. 'I just wanted to spend some time with my daughter,' he said, hating the weakness, the vulnerability in his voice. 'I know you might not credit me with this, but the moment I saw our daughter, that is how I felt. Terrified that you would take her away from me. That I would never have access to her. The reason I want us to marry is so that we have *equal* rights. Not because I want sole custody. I am not so much of a monster that I would rip my daughter away from her mother.'

'As you intended when you came to my bed and breakfast and tried to take my daughter from me?'

'As I intended when I thought that the mother of my child was an alcoholic, willing to use my child to blackmail me for money, a mother who I thought— *at that time*—was a threat to my daughter's safety.' Dimitri ran a hand over his face. This wasn't getting them anywhere. 'Please, let me call a doctor for you. That was a really hard fall.'

Anna looked at him accusingly. As if the fall had been his fault. As if this whole sorry mess was his fault. And he had to acknowledge the truth of it. He followed her gaze as she turned her attention to Amalia outside with Flora.

'I didn't know what to do when she started crying,' he confessed. 'She'd been so quiet and happy until…'

'She's good with strangers because of the bed and breakfast. She's used to seeing different faces.'

Dimitri couldn't stop the anger that rose within him quickly and eagerly, eating up the space that she had given him.

'I'm not a stranger, Anna.'

'Oh,' she retorted with fake surprise. 'Have you explained that to our twenty-seven-month-old daughter? She's bright, but genetics may be a little above her age range.'

He barely restrained the growl that almost choked him.

Anna stood on still shaking legs. 'I'm going to go and take a shower.' Dimitri watched her struggle to get to her feet for barely a second before he stood and swept her into his arms. He'd done that the night they'd come together and had forgotten how impossibly light she was.

'What are you doing?'

'Am I hurting you?' he asked, before taking another step.

'No,' she said into his chest. Instead of pulling away, as he had expected her to do, she leaned into him just a little, and he ignored the shift that he felt beneath his ribcage, pushing away the swift and sudden arousal that had caught him by surprise. She must have been in considerable pain. He'd seen American football players take less hard hits than she had. That was what he told his mind, but his body seemed to have its own thoughts.

He was only wearing a thin T-shirt, the temperature in Greece considerably hotter than the cold dampness of Ireland that had seeped into his bones and not let go until he'd returned Anna and his— *their*—daughter to his home on this island. The thin material offered no protection against the feeling of her skin against his. Everything in him screamed at him to take her straight to his bed, but he wasn't that much of a bastard.

He walked back up the stairs to her room and gently slid her down the full length of his body, torturing himself, punishing himself with what he could not have, and settled her gently on the floor.

His arms were still around her and she looked up at him, the golden flecks in her large green eyes flaring. Their breaths caught at the same time. He was chest-to-chest with her, barely an inch between them. It was the closest they'd been since that night.

As she exhaled, he breathed in deeply, and he was half convinced that he could taste her on his tongue. It would take nothing at all to close the distance, to take her lips as his traitorous body had wanted to do since he'd laid eyes on her just those few days ago in Ireland. Need coursed through his veins with lightning speed, tightening muscles all over his body.

And in her eyes, he could see it too, that need, that want. Anna's breathing became light little puffs of air against his cheek, ratcheting up his arousal to impossible heights. Begging, pleading almost for him to take her.

His fingers gripped and flexed, trying to find the space where skin met skin and, instead of letting her go as his mind was shouting at him to, he pulled her closer, the inch of air between them became a centimetre and…

'I should have that shower.'

When she looked back at him some of the anger, the pain had returned to her eyes and somehow he forced his body to let her go. He straightened and walked away, out of the room, out of the house, and kept on walking until he had his body under control once more.

Anna woke for the second time that day, disorientated and—this time—in pain. Her leg throbbed and her shoulder and arm hurt from where she'd tried to break her fall. As she rose to get up from the bed Flora came in, her arms flapping and a string of Greek accompanying the glass of water and painkillers she thrust into her hands.

Anna took them and drank down the water thankfully. Slowly she tried to get up again and this time succeeded. From the time on the clock, she'd hoped that her daughter would have been put down for her nap. As she looked into the room, Amalia's soft little breaths assured her that she was okay. She made her way back down to the kitchen area, and asked Flora where Dimitri was. The older woman scowled and with a shrugging of her shoulders went back to preparing a feast fit for a king.

She was in Greece, it struck her fully for the first time. After Dimitri had told her that she wouldn't get their passports back unless she married him, it had short-circuited all thoughts about the incredible place he had brought them to.

Once again she felt adrift. She watched on helplessly as Flora pottered around the kitchen, occasionally bringing delicious things for her to try. And, as much as she wanted to be excited by the lovely food, she longed for the time when, only yesterday, she would have been able to go to her fridge and prepare lunch with the things that she and Amalia were used to eating. And then she felt ungrateful. Not to Dimitri, but to Flora, who was becoming increasingly attentive the more uncomfortable Anna was feeling.

Dimitri came in from the pool area, looking windswept and mouthwateringly handsome. He had changed from the T-shirt he'd been wearing earlier in the day and replaced it with a white linen shirt that hung slightly open at the neck showing swirls of dark hair on his chest. Just a brief foray out into the sunshine had turned his skin a golden brown, and his dark eyes, heavy with concern, poked and prodded at the memory of the moment they had shared just before her shower. His hands were jammed into the pockets of his tan trousers, and bare feet padded their way towards her.

Anna felt a blush rise to her cheeks. She would have kissed him. The man who had brought her to Greece and taken away her freedom. The man who was threatening to keep her daughter here without her permission.

'Flora, this smells delicious,' he said in English, clearly for her benefit.

Flora grunted in response, shrugging her shoulders at him, the way she had done when Anna had asked after him earlier. Anna just about raised a smile for the female solidarity in the kitchen.

'How are you feeling?' he asked her. As stubborn as she had a mind to be, she couldn't ignore him completely. Even Flora seemed to hold her breath to see if she would answer him.

'Stiff. Sore. But okay,' she said eventually and Flora turned her attention back to pulling a tray of roast tomatoes from the oven.

'Have you been awake long?'

'Not very. Flora has been taking care of me,' she said, smiling over at the housekeeper, who had taken to humming along to herself while she cooked. She pressed two glasses of cold white wine in their direction. Anna frowned. 'I'm not sure that's a good idea. I've just taken two painkillers.'

Flora hushed her and said something in Greek, which Dimitri translated. 'She says it's fine, you've only had ibuprofen. A little wine won't hurt.' He paused and smiled as Flora continued. 'She said you need to relax.'

Anna let out a huff at that. Dimitri picked up the two glasses of wine and gestured for her to follow him outside. Flora caught her casting a worried glance up at her daughter's room, and with a *'Nai, nai, nai,'* she shooed her outside after Dimitri.

The view that she walked out to was breathtaking. A pergola spread out from the sides of the house, where beautiful tendrils of pink bougainvillea picked up the last rays of the sun as it sank into the welcome arms of the horizon. To her left an infinity pool stretched out towards the sea. Only the pool tiles gave the water a slightly lighter shade of aquamarine, allowing her to pick out the edge of the patio and the start of the sea beyond it.

Dimitri pressed a glass slick with condensation into her hands. The cool drink would be a welcome relief from the heat of the day. But she couldn't quite bring herself to take a sip of the light-coloured liquid.

She needed to find the strength to ask the questions that had been crying out in her mind since the night before. Since he'd made that awful demand.

'I do want you to know your daughter. Really I do. But I don't understand why I have to marry you in order for that to happen.' She ignored the darkening of his eyes and pressed on. 'I'd be happy to amend the birth certificate, I'd be happy to discuss joint custody—'

'It's not enough,' Dimitri ground out, trying to suppress the rage he felt. Knowing that it had as much to do with the present as it did the past. 'All that legal wrangling…if something happened to me, or if something happened to *you*, I would not want my child's future to be dependent on lawyers.'

'Dimitri, nothing's going to—'

'You don't know that!' he barked, cursing himself for his loss of control. 'You cannot know that, Anna. I was only seven years old when my mother died.' His own words had shocked him. He'd had no intention of revealing his past, but now that he'd started he couldn't seem to stop. 'She'd been in a car accident on the way back from her shift as a waitress in the local restaurant. I'd come home from school, was watching TV, when the police knocked on the door.' In his mind he was back in their small one-bedroom apartment in Piraeus, the sound of the fist against wood something he'd never forget. Ever. His memories skipped over the moment of shock, of pain… and instead called to his mind the confusion…of not knowing what would happen. Of being numb to almost everything, even his grief, other than the fear of what would happen to him now. 'It took my mother's sister two months to track my father down. The father I'd never met before. A family I knew nothing about and who, aside from my father, knew nothing about me.' He'd been thrust into a world of impossible money and luxury, where the corridors echoed with arguments, and shouts, always accompanied by his name.

'So yes, Anna, we might not know each other, and yes, marriage might seem extreme to you, but you will marry me because I know that you'll do what's needed to protect our child.'

She had watched him with solemn eyes and he turned away as something horrifyingly like pity shone there.

'I know—'

He couldn't prevent the dismissive huff that fell from his lips as he turned back to her.

'I know,' she repeated, 'how important that is… My father was… My father left us before I was born.'

'Then you understand why we must marry.'

Anna shook her head sadly, the long, dark, layered tendrils of her hair framing her face and shoulders. 'Dimitri, your father wasn't married to your mother, yet he took you in. My father *was* married to my mother and it didn't stop him from leaving us.'

Dimitri frowned, remembering his investigator's report on Mary Moore. 'But there is no father named on your birth certificate.'

'It was the only way my mother could find to hurt him the way he'd hurt her. And before you ask,' she said, throwing up a hand between them as if to ward off an attack she'd known would come, 'I couldn't have put you on Amalia's birth certificate without you being there. And you were…'

'In prison.'

She nodded. 'I'd like some time to think about this. Perhaps we could talk tomorrow?'

Dimitri's jaw clenched as he remembered what tomorrow would bring.

'Sadly I don't think that will happen. Tomorrow we have a family party to go to.'

The next morning Anna found herself wearing a sumptuous silk dress that would have kept the bed and breakfast away from the bank manager for at least two more months. The dress had appeared in her room as if magicked there by fairies—though, in reality, probably just by a very well-paid assistant. She, Amalia and Dimitri had been swept up in yet another limousine from Piraeus after the short boat ride from the island, and she was now staring, wide-eyed, as the limo pulled up the drive of one of the biggest villas she had ever seen.

If Dimitri had been concerned by the press lining the street outside his family's home, he hadn't shown it. Her eyes still stung from the camera flashes, even through the tinted windows. Her ears still hurt from the yells, demands for a sound bite, even though she'd not understood the Greek words.

But all of that was pushed aside by the sheer magnitude of the Kyriakou estate. To say it was enormous would have been a gross understatement. But she couldn't help but find the ostentatiousness slightly distasteful. Calling to mind Dimitri's words from the night before, she wondered how this must have been to a little boy whose mother had worked as a waitress. The loss he must have felt at such a young age... The thought of it made her chest ache. Her heart. She couldn't even begin to imagine it.

'This is where you grew up?' she asked Dimitri, unable to hide the awe in her voice. 'After leaving your mother's?' She waited so long for an answer, she was unbuckling Amalia from her seat when she heard his reply.

'Yes.'

By the time she had retrieved Amalia from the car, Dimitri was standing beside a brand-new pushchair she had once lusted after. A pushchair that had felt a million miles out of her reach but had been obtained with less than a blink of Dimitri's dark eyes.

Amalia was struggling in her arms, refusing to get into it.

'It's okay. You're better off carrying her anyway,' Dimitri stated. 'My family will want to pass her around. I hope that you're okay with that?'

The tone of his voice issued a challenge she knew she had no hope of winning. And besides, this was why she had come to Greece, she reminded herself. To allow Amalia to get to know her family. Of course, that was before she had been threatened with blackmail to marry a man she hardly knew but was beginning to see glimpses of. So much had happened in the last twenty-four hours, it was hard to focus on that salient event. And today, she was supposed to smile and lie to that same family about what she was doing in Greece.

She hadn't even agreed to his demands yet, but sensed that he, as with all else, simply expected her compliance. Anna felt swept along by the tidal wave that was *Dimitri*. With no choice, no decision-making necessary, all she could do was hope to come out the other end able to breathe.

She followed him up the stone stairs that led to an impressive set of large doors, open on their hinges. A wall of cool air hit her the moment she stepped over the threshold, as did the sounds of a large outdoor party in full swing. They passed through a cream marble foyer, with room after room shooting off the corridor, each decorated in styles that ranged from tasteful to outrageous. But it was when they reached the doorway to the garden that her feet slowed to a stop. Even Amalia had stopped wriggling. Anna tried to prevent the gasp that fell from her lips, but clearly failed. It was like a scene from a magazine spread of the rich and famous—only she didn't recognise any of the people.

A tall, thin, attractive woman approached with a wide smile and a twinkle in her eye. She introduced herself as Nella, Dimitri's cousin, and drew them towards a circle of women and children sitting under a large white awning.

Within seconds, the whole of Dimitri's family had descended upon them, all speaking at the same time, pinching cheeks, giving hugs, and a litany of comments in both English and Greek complaining of how skinny both Anna and Amalia were. Amalia was quickly removed from her embrace and replaced with a plate of food and a glass of wine.

Even though Dimitri stood behind her, silent and brooding, as if reluctant to let them out of his sight, Anna couldn't help but smile as her daughter lapped up the attention lavished upon her, while she answered yet another question about why she didn't have red hair or pale skin. *Yes*, she was Irish, but she was *also* Vietnamese. Unsurprisingly this didn't seem to help the confusion much. *No*, she couldn't possibly eat another bite; she was almost popping out of the brand-new dress. As would Amalia, if she wasn't careful.

In a small corner of her heart, Anna had to acknowledge that everyone was lovely and welcoming. All the aunts and uncles, cousins and children were loud and brash and exactly how she'd once wanted Amalia's family to be. With a few glances at his chiselled profile she stuck to the story that Dimitri had woven from the space in between truth and fiction: that they had met three years ago and had wanted to keep their relationship quiet because of the legal problems. She voiced the lies time and time again because his family all seemed so hopeful that something good had come from such a difficult time.

Anna had never really given much thought to the ramifications of Dimitri's half-brother's actions. She hadn't even had the chance to find out what *he* felt about the whole thing. What that kind of betrayal must have done to him. That thought probed painfully at the thin layer of guilt hiding beneath the outrage she struggled with from his high-handedness.

Dimitri's cousin Nella drew her back from her thoughts by telling her that she was too pale, that she needed more sun to make her skin shine. Whether it was because she had spent years hating the very thing that had marked her as so different in Ireland, or whether it was because she liked the straight-talking Greek girl, she promised herself that she would make an effort with Nella, as something about her made her think that they could be really good friends.

Seeing Anna tucked safely under the wing of his cousin, Dimitri turned to observe the rest of the party, trying to see it with fresh eyes. Women in richly coloured clothes—turquoise, red, white, royal blue—assaulted the eyes, but not as much as the incredible amount of expensive jewellery that hung around necks, dripped from ears and fingers. Deeply tanned men in linen suits wore watches that screamed money, sunglasses that hid boredom or jealousy, or both.

He'd recognised Anna's initial look of wonder, curiosity and even a little bit of fear and with an amused laugh he didn't really feel, he realised that he must have looked like that the first time he'd come here.

'Is it hard being back here after what happened with your brother?'

He hadn't realised that Anna had stopped speaking with Nella and come to stand beside him.

'Half-brother,' Dimitri instantly replied. As if that made it more understandable. As if that made the betrayal somehow less. He hadn't wanted to admit to her that this was the first time since Manos's arrest that he'd been home. The first time that he'd seen his father and stepmother in person. It was a weakness, and he hated it.

Only his father could throw such a lavish party in the face of such an enormous family scandal and get away with it. Nowhere on the faces of the guests did he see concern or embarrassment. The only intrigue came from the rabid reporters clamouring at the gates. And he wondered if it was exactly this kind of self-delusion, this ability to ignore something so wrong, that had allowed Manos to get away with what he did.

A waiter passed with a tray of champagne flutes, and, unthinking, he took one and drank down half of the serving. When Anna politely declined he raised an eyebrow, forgetting that she couldn't see it behind the large frames of his sunglasses.

'You can drink if you want. I'll only be having this one.' He needed all his wits about him with the exchange he was about to have with his father.

'That's okay, I don't really drink.'

Of course she wouldn't. Mary Moore had probably seen to that. But then the memory of their first night together surfaced again, unbidden. The taste of whisky on her lips, unable to mask the sweetness of her mouth.

'When we met—'

'Darling,' a voice interrupted his train of thought. 'You're here,' scolded Eleni Kyriakou in English, as if they hadn't already been here some time. And 'darling'? When had she ever called him that? he wondered, not even bothering to scour his memory. He turned to take in the vivid array of patterned silks that adorned his stepmother. There was an almost forced happiness in her eyes—as if that could cover the deep discomfort they had both felt long before Manos's arrest.

'Eleni,' he acknowledged, knowing that it was better to meet her head-on than avoid her.

'And this,' she said with more warmth than he'd ever heard before, 'must be Amalia. My beautiful granddaughter.'

Dimitri scanned Anna's face for any signs that she might have been upset by the subtle snub, but her features were schooled. Good. She'd need to keep them that way if she was to survive this afternoon.

Guilty. When was he going to stop feeling guilty? *Christe mou*, perhaps he was the one who needed to toughen up. He was doing what he had to in order to claim his child. Anna had made decisions that had brought this upon herself. That was what he needed to remind himself. His only interest in her went as far as 'I do', and nothing further.

Before he could stop her, Eleni was reaching out to take Amalia from Anna's hands and he saw the brief flash of something pass across Anna's eyes, but Eleni was so focused on their child she missed it. Assuring himself once more that Anna would be just fine, he extricated himself from the situation and went in search of Agapetos Kyriakou, his father.

Swift, powerful steps took him back into the house that held such painful memories. He'd been putting off this confrontation for as long as possible, but now…it couldn't be avoided. He wasn't surprised to find his father in the study, but he *was* surprised to hear his lawyer David's clipped British accent coming from the speaker phone.

'I refuse to discuss this without my client present.'

'I'm here,' Dimitri ground out, stepping into the room, clearly surprising the two men attempting to go behind his back. 'What is going on?'

His father at least had the grace to look discomfited, which was about as far as Agapetos had ever managed in his presence. Nikos, his father's lawyer, launched into a fast-paced litany of Dimitri's errors, but he interrupted.

'English, please. David doesn't speak Greek.'

'And that is your fault for hiring an English lawyer,' Nikos bit back in English, his father staying silent for once.

'What did he say?' David asked through the phone's speaker.

'Nikos was calling me seven shades of a fool for not having a DNA test done before bringing Anna and Amalia here,' Dimitri explained, the fury he felt making his tone harsh. 'I will make this clear once and for all. I would *never* allow my child to grow up knowing that her place with me was determined only by a positive test. Or growing up thinking that she's only worth her DNA.'

'Then you *are* a fool,' stated Nikos.

'She is my daughter. I know it. And, as her father, it's my job to protect her from pain. Whether financial *or* emotional.'

Nikos looked as if he was about to reply, when his father cut him off.

'If my son says that she is his, then she is his.'

It was as if a bucket of ice-cold water had been thrown over him. The hairs rose on his arms, and breath locked in his lungs. Never, *ever* had his father shown such confidence in him before. He stared at Agapetos, though the older man refused to meet his gaze, whether from discomfort at the emotional statement, or… Dimitri didn't know what else it could have been. His entire life he'd been waiting, hoping for a sign of kindness, affection, even just support from his father, and it happened now? Did he feel guilty over Manos's actions?

'Leave us,' Agapetos ordered his lawyer. There was a brief battle of wills, but eventually Nikos left the room, leaving him alone with his father. Feeling as if the ground had shifted beneath him, Dimitri waited.

'You will marry her?'

'I'm doing everything in my power to ensure that happens.'

'Good. That is good.'

Dimitri frowned. He'd expected his father to say the words Nikos had uttered, not this. Not his desire to see him married with a child.

'I'd...' His father took a deep breath and pressed on. 'I'd like to see this as a new beginning. A fresh start...for all of us. Anna and Amalia included. I'm not saying it will be easy, but I'd like to try.'

Dimitri could only nod, as his father swept an arm over his shoulder the way he had seen him do with Manos time and time again.

'Then I'd like, very much, to see my granddaughter.'

Anna watched the two men leave the room from the shadowed enclave beside the study. She had gone in search of Dimitri after feeling his absence too long and had paused the moment she'd heard David's voice on the phone asking what was being said.

She had listened, her heart in her mouth at Dimitri's simple words, his resolute defiance of the man he called Nikos... They had struck her as something incredible. There was so much loaded into Dimitri's response, Anna struggled to unpick it. His love for his child and the trust he had in her, trust that she had taken for granted. He'd asked her only once if Amalia was his daughter. That was all it had taken.

She wanted that for Amalia. A father who would

care for her, protect her, stand up for her. Again, the bittersweet slice of pain each time Dimitri said or did something good reminded her of the lack that she had grown up with. She knew how easy it was for a father to turn away from his child, to fail in that one duty, even to replace that child with another family...

As Dimitri's wife, that wouldn't happen. As Dimitri's wife, she would be ensuring that her daughter was protected, cared for and loved even. She might not be able to expect those things for herself, but she *would* secure them for her daughter. What she would, however, secure for herself was protection. For her heart.

CHAPTER FIVE

Dear Dimitri,
Today I made a deal with the devil.

DIMITRI PACED THE length of the patio, moonlight his
only companion as Anna settled their daughter in
her bedroom. He knew that she had something on
her mind, having been quiet the entire journey back
from his father's house. And that suited him fine.
He was still reeling from his father's behaviour.
He had cooed over his grandchild in a way Dimitri
never imagined Agapetos had done with either him
or Manos. Was it possible that they could have the
fresh start his father had promised? Could he forgive
the hurts of the past? Could he push away the difficult memories and feelings that he associated with
his father, his childhood?

Anna came out onto the patio and hovered behind
a seat at the large handcrafted table he'd bought from
one of the local tradesmen. He watched as she ran her
fingers over the fine grain of the wood, the moonlight glinting off the slight curls in her long, dark hair.

'I...' She paused, seeming to struggle over what she had to say. She pressed on again. 'I will marry you.'

It was not what he'd expected. In fact, he had returned to the house, ready to counter her objection to marrying him with more threats and more anger. So it took Dimitri a moment to catch up with the elation that was coursing through his body.

'But I have a few conditions.'

This was a different Anna to the one who had sat in the small staff area of her B & B, the one who couldn't meet his eyes. This Anna was the Anna he'd met that night three years before. Calm, assessing, in control. As if muscle memory moved within him, the taste of arousal pierced his tongue. She was glorious again. He wasn't concerned about her conditions, but he would let her voice them. Negotiation was about give and take. But what she didn't yet know was that Dimitri intended to take everything that he wanted.

'We need to agree to stop all the games. All the blackmail.'

'*Nai*—yes. This can be done.'

'I'll sign a prenup. Whatever you need. But I want to move forward from a place of equality. You have—' she paused infinitesimally '—all the power. And that's not okay. I am Amalia's mother. If we marry, you will never have sole custody of my child.'

'Understood. And agreed.'

'If the current caretakers of the bed and breakfast prove themselves, and if they are happy to do so, they can continue in my absence until we hear what my mother would like to do with the business. Until then, Amalia and I will stay here in Greece.'

'Good.'

'I want to be able to visit Ireland and spend time there each year.'

'Absolutely. It's important that all aspects of her heritage are available to her. I will have brochures of possible homes here by the morning.'

'I want to learn Greek,' she said, taking him by surprise. 'I won't be cut out from conversations between you and my daughter. This marriage will only work if we communicate openly.'

'We will find someone right away.' Why was she agreeing so suddenly? Where was the catch?

'And...' Was that a blush he could see paint her cheeks? 'And I will not be sharing a bed with you.'

'What?'

'This will be a marriage on paper, one with legal rights, but I will not share your bed.'

'You expect me to live like a monk, and you a nun?' he demanded, his body crying out to reject her preposterous stipulation.

'I have very few expectations of you, Dimitri. I just don't want to find out about it. The possibility of it is one thing, but knowing it? I'd rather not.'

That cut him deeply. He had never made claims of sainthood and certainly had his fair share of experience, but he would never treat his wife the way his father had treated either his stepmother or his own mother.

'Hear me now, Anna. I would never disrespect my wife, or the mother of my child in that way. Ever.' His words were binding, the promise ringing in his own ears. If Anna was taken aback by the vehemence in his tone, Dimitri didn't see it. 'But if you think this marriage will be left outside the bedroom, you are very much mistaken.'

He wanted, so much, to go to her, to lean into the area of heat surrounding her body. To relish it. But he didn't. He left the table between them, allowed her the space and clarity to fully understand his words. But despite the distance, desire was thick on the air around them and the little flare of the pulse at her neck told him all he needed to know.

'I won't sleep with you,' she whispered, her voice trembling as she struggled to hide her attraction to him.

'You would deny yourself the pleasure we shared? I still remember the cries of your ecstasy as you came apart in my arms. As you begged me for more. Deeper, harder, again and again. The way your eyes opened as I met every single one of your requests.'

The way her eyes opened now, wide but unseeing, lost in the memory his words had conjured, her sharp inhale as her body swayed towards him. His own arousal was painfully hard, pressing against the material of his trousers, and the sight of her own desire, the way her nipples had hardened, peaked against the thin silk of her dress, was the only satisfaction he had at that moment.

'Tell me, Anna… Do *you* remember?'

* * *

She inwardly cursed as a shaky breath left her lungs, feeling it was as much an answer as he needed. *Of course* she remembered. His simple words had plunged her into an arousal that she felt in every single part of her body. The present clashed with the past as she felt his caress on her skin, relished the memory of him within her, filling her, completing her in a way she had never imagined. She felt now her skin flush, her erratic heartbeat flutter, even though he was still standing on the other side of the table. She hated that her body made a mockery of her words. Betraying her in the most fundamental way.

Yes, she wanted to cry. She *did* remember. She *did* want to reach out, to touch him, feel the weight of his punishing kisses, the way that only he made her body come alive. But it was the greater risk, the one to her heart, that she was truly fearful of. And *that* was why she couldn't let herself be with him. She couldn't let him in at all. Because if she did, she wasn't sure that she would survive it.

'I will make you this promise, Anna.' His voice called to her as she struggled with the intoxicating feelings of her desire. 'I will not seduce you with fine words and wine, I will not come to your door. Not once. And I will *not* touch you against your will.'

Anna jerked a breath of air into her lungs—had she done it? Had she got him to agree to her condition?

'I won't have to.' Dimitri pulled his head back, just enough to meet her eyes. '*You* will come to me.

You will beg *me* to touch you. To take you as I did that night, over and over again. You will plead with me to pleasure you, to find the release that only I have given you. And I will, Anna. I assure you that I will. But *you* will be the one to come to *me*.'

Weeks slipped through Anna's fingers like sand. She had settled into a strange routine with Dimitri, who spent his mornings with her and Amalia at breakfast, and returned after the sun had set. She had learned to both long for and resent those hours. He hovered in the background as if he were some dark angel, waiting for her to make a mistake. He was there with her when her daughter woke in the night, watching her soothe Amalia's tears. He shared Anna's joy as Amalia would race along the patio, holding herself up at the plastic railing fencing off the swimming pool.

Occasionally he would surprise her with a visit in the afternoon, a brief swim with Amalia as she splashed and giggled in the water. But when Amalia was asleep he was there, waiting for Anna to come to him. She resented the sense of satisfaction she felt coming off him in waves whenever he was near, as if he smugly knew more about herself, her body, than she did.

Each night she would lie awake, listening to the quiet house, imagining him in his bed, the sound of his breathing, the slip-slide of his skin against his sheets. It was a slow torture as she fell into fevered dreams of his body, his touch, his caress, the feel of him moving deep within her. And each morning she woke more exhausted than the day before. He had stayed true to his promise. He had not touched her, nor come to her, but she felt as if she was being watched, hunted, slowly entrapped by her own desires.

Anna put the phone back in its cradle. Her mother's therapist had informed her that Mary had requested to stay on yet another month, refusing contact with Anna even though she was entitled to that now. It hurt and it surprised her to find that her mother still had access to parts of her heart that would cause such pain.

But she wanted to let her mother know about her marriage personally, rather than reading about it in the headlines of a newspaper. The therapist had agreed to pass on a letter, should Mary Moore feel up to reading it.

That she wouldn't be at the wedding…well. Anna still couldn't quite tell how she felt about it. She thought of the wedding more in an abstract way, as if it was something simply to be done. An event to be planned, rather than a marriage or a future way of life.

But as she began the letter, her hand automatically began to spell out Dimitri's name…and she thought of the hundreds of pages she had written to him over the years, telling him of something Amalia had done, telling him of the joys and the tears she had shed, Amalia's first bath, first steps, first words, first smile, second teeth and second words, second falls and third. To tell him of the moment she had truly realised that she was a mother. The well of love that had almost brought her to her knees. All of that she had wanted to share with the father of her child. But the man she was marrying? He was not the same man she had written to over the last few years. She needed to be realistic. Now, more than ever, was not the time for fantasies and could-have-beens.

Pushing thoughts aside, she focused on the letter in front of her. Anna's hands shook a little as she committed the words to the page.

Dear Ma,
I'm getting married... I have decided to stay in Greece. The lovely couple running the bed and breakfast are taking good care of it for us. You'd like them, Ma.
I wish you could see Dimitri's house. It's incredible. One day I hope that you will. Amalia is getting big! She's outgrown almost all of the clothes I brought with us.
And I've been learning a little Greek. Flora, Dimitri's housekeeper, has been teaching me a phrase a day, along with some of the most delicious recipes...

Dimitri paced the length of his Athens office. How was it that, on the cusp of achieving everything he had wanted, he suddenly felt trapped? Trapped by the marriage he had brought upon himself. He cursed out loud into the empty room, the words bouncing off the sleek chrome and dark wood that surrounded him. When he had been in prison, he had longed to come back to his office. The place where he was in control. He had longed to stand once again in his house, looking out on to the open sea, but somehow he couldn't shake the feeling that he had swapped one cage for another.

He rubbed at his ring finger, the phantom itch that had started the moment that Anna had agreed to his proposal. What did he know about marriage? His own father had been a bastard and had abandoned his mother, the young waitress he had ruthlessly seduced, then discarded, just like he had his son. Even if he had softened at the party just weeks ago, Dimitri couldn't ignore the way he had been his entire life until that point. Agapetos's own marriage had been based solely on a business deal, rather than any finer feelings, and it had kept his entire family in a state of misery throughout Dimitri's life. Was that what would become of him and Anna? Would she come to resent him for forcing this upon them? Would *he*?

He was no better off than when he was stuck in that prison, where testosterone mixed with anger, impotence and helplessness. Where desperation made men weak, and bullies strong. Where fear was a feral animal stalking the hallways, beaten, bruised and bloodied.

His only release was the short moments he would steal with his daughter. Her laughter was a panacea to the chaotic thoughts that filtered through his mind almost constantly. Whether it was breakfast, where

Amalia would rain down an Armageddon of culinary destruction, or the evenings, where he would watch over Anna as she soothed her daughter's night-time tears, he still felt like an outsider. But the thing that had surprised him the most was the fear of somehow causing damage to the small life they had created together.

He couldn't turn to Agapetos, couldn't trust the fragile bond that had begun to form with his offering of peace. He couldn't turn to Antonio and Danyl, who hadn't the first clue of parenting. Antonio was busy making plans for his wedding to Emma. Danyl had the weight of an entire country on his shoulders, and Dimitri was reluctant to add to that. No. To all intents and purposes, Dimitri was alone in this. And that was the only real way he knew how to be. He had long since learned that he couldn't rely on others to help bear his burden. So instead, he became a man on the verge of the perfect marriage to the mother of his child. That was the image he needed to maintain, and perhaps if he told himself that enough times he might start believing it.

'Mr Kyriakou?' The intercom buzzed with his new assistant's voice. 'The Sheikh of Ter'harn and Antonio Arcuri are here to see you.'

Before she had even finished speaking, Danyl had stormed into his office, laden with two bottles of dark amber liquid in each hand, Antonio swiftly following behind.

'You didn't think you could get married and miss out on the stag, did you?'

* * *

The doorbell rang just as Anna put the letter to her mother in an envelope. Flora had offered to post it for her, Anna's limited Greek most definitely *not* up for ensuring its secure delivery. The sound of voices from the hallway and an unaccountably flustered Flora surprised her. Frowning, Anna rounded the corner to see Dimitri's stepmother, Eleni, in the doorway, with what looked like an army of people and clothes behind her.

'Mrs Kyriakou?' asked Anna, unaware of her plans to visit.

'Ms Moore,' she said, still failing to make eye contact as she brushed a piece of imaginary lint from her chic designer suit.

'Anna, please call me Anna' was all she could reply as Eleni Kyriakou pushed her way into the house that suddenly felt a million times smaller as it filled with uniformed people dragging racks of covered dresses into the open-plan living area.

'Anna,' Eleni finally relented. If there was a superior 'sniff' to be heard, Anna was sure it was covered by the cacophony of voices that filled the room.

Amalia stirred in her high chair at the table, craning her neck to take in what new exciting delights had surrounded her. In an instant, all the formidable uniformed minions turned into gushing women, pinching her cheeks and thighs and exclaiming happily in Greek. Flora descended, shooing them away, retrieving Amalia and sending Anna a look that told her categorically that she wasn't paid enough to deal with Eleni Kyriakou.

Eleni looked longingly after her granddaughter and Anna felt a little burst of pity for the older woman. Until she turned her assessing gaze on Anna.

'You are in need of a dress, I believe,' the older woman stated. Anna took a closer inspection of the covered garments on the racks. Wedding dresses.

It wasn't as if Anna had ever really imagined her wedding day, what she would be wearing, or how— even—she would be choosing the dress, but it had never involved the overbearing stepmother of Dimitri Kyriakou. In fact, Anna had thought that perhaps she might spend the day in Athens and pick something from a retail store. But the names in gilt lettering on the covers of these dresses were some of the most expensive designers she had ever heard of. And then there were names of designers she hadn't heard of, whose clothes were guaranteed to be priceless.

Within seconds she was being manhandled out of her light clothes, and standing before her soon-to-be mother-in-law in little more than her underwear. Anna knew that her body had regained her pre-baby figure fairly easily after a diet of sleepless nights and hard working hours at the bed and breakfast, but still she seemed only just to pass muster.

The dispassionate assessment of her physique made her feel like a mannequin, as gown after gown was relieved of its covering. The sheer number of dresses and styles almost overwhelmed her, although some called for instant dismissal, especially the one that made her think of Little Bo Peep. Taffeta was discarded as impossible, tulle too heavy for the heat and, although Anna was surprised to find herself quite liking the shorter, nineteen-fifties-style skirt, Eleni Kyriakou dismissed it with a flick of her red nail-polished finger. Finally one of the younger stylists timidly brought forward her offering while the others were distracted. She cast one quick glance in their direction, before pressing it into Anna's hands and shooing her off behind the screen that had been erected in the living room for what little was left of her modesty.

As her fingers reached out to the exquisite lace detail of the plunging bodice, a thread of excitement wound through her. The skirt was long, and pure oyster-coloured silk, flaring out into a seamless fishtail. Exquisite lace detail was sewn onto the barely visible material of sleeves that would cover her arms down to her wrists. Anna almost groaned out loud when she saw the hundreds of little buttons at the back but was pleasantly surprised to find a concealed zip hidden beneath them. She stepped into the cool, silky skirt and lifted the bodice over her breasts, realising that she'd have to discard her bra.

As she pulled the zip, she cast a glance at her reflection in the window—the nearest mirror was in the hallway. The bodice lay flat against her stomach, and the plunging neckline revealed enough to be sexy but hid enough to be respectable. Her sunbronzed skin glowed against the oyster colour of the silk. She swept her hair up in a band and a spark of excitement ignited within her. *This* was the one. She knew it. She could feel the rightness of it settle about her as the silk skirts swirled about her bare feet.

Tentatively she stepped out from behind the screen, just in time to see Flora, returning to the house with Amalia, stop dead in her tracks. All conversation in the room halted midsentence. For a second Anna worried that she'd made a huge mistake, until everyone started talking at once, oohing and aahing after the gown.

Anna felt a smile spread over her mouth, and even Eleni appeared to be satisfied.

After the assistants had removed all the dresses from Dimitri's house and Anna was back in her own clothes, she sat at the table to have coffee with Flora and Eleni. Anna had expected Eleni to leave with the magic she'd summoned that morning, but she hadn't.

'Your mother?' Eleni asked her, slightly uncomfortably. 'She is not able to come?'

'No, she's…she's having medical treatment.'

'And your friends?'

Anna didn't really want to explain how she couldn't have asked the few friends that had survived her job and her child to pay for the extraordinarily expensive air fare to Greece in the summer months. Nor how she would have explained to them the events of the last few weeks.

Eleni nodded as if she somehow understood. 'Nella, Dimitri's cousin, told me that the English have a tradition in weddings. I'm not sure if it's the same for Ireland…' Anna was too busy wondering when her English had got so good to try to understand where this was going. Eleni looked to Flora. It was the first time that Anna had seen her anything less than poised and, well, rude, frankly.

'Something old, something borrowed...' said Eleni, producing the most exquisite pearl-encrusted bracelet. The colour of the pearls matched her dress perfectly, and Anna felt the stir of emotion within her breast.

'New and blue,' Flora said, less articulately, placing a beautiful blue lacy garter beside the pearls.

Anna was overcome in an instant. She felt tears pressing against her eyes. It was a silly tradition, one she hadn't even given a second thought to, but that these two women had made such an effort to make it happen... She felt so grateful to Nella for thinking of such a thing, and somehow managing to convince Eleni to be part of it. Around the table sat three generations of women, all brought together by Dimitri, and Anna, who had not once felt that kind of female solidarity or emotional support before, was so very touched.

'Not all weddings...start the same way,' Eleni said, still not quite able to make eye contact with her. 'But Dimitri, he is a good man. He will care for you and your child.' Her words soothed Anna's unspoken fears, just a little, and made Anna wonder at Eleni's own marriage. 'We do what we have to, for our children, *nai*?'

Eleni's burst of honesty made Anna bold. 'Does Dimitri know that you think he is a good man?'

Eleni paused before continuing, clearly wondering how much to reveal of their relationship.

'Dimitri's childhood with us was…not easy. His father is…*not* easy,' she said honestly. 'It may have been easier for Dimitri to see me as…as…' she seemed to be struggling, whether with the English language, or something far harder '…very different to his own mother. And when he came to us I was worried about my own son, Manos. And now with what has happened…'

Flora's tutting interrupted Eleni, who shot a dark look at the older woman. No matter what her son had done, and how he had done it, Eleni was still his mother. Anna knew that bond. Knew what she would do for her daughter.

'But there is a goodness in Dimitri. I know that.'

Anna could only hope that Eleni was right. Because she was about to commit her life and her daughter to Dimitri Kyriakou.

CHAPTER SIX

Dear Dimitri,
Today I wore your ring.

THE CHURCH WHERE they were to be married was like something out of a film. It was on a small jut of land reaching out to the sea, accessible only during low tide. The small building's roughly hewn hunks of blondstone melted into the sand behind it and were surrounded by sea and sky.

The late afternoon sun still providing a pure golden light and heat, the way it never did in Ireland, made Anna feel as if it were something from a dream rather than the day that she committed her life to Dimitri.

Because the church was so small and the number of guests so large, the wedding was held outside, in front of the old building. A large erected awning provided guests with shelter from the blaze of the sun. Rows and rows of chairs had been placed in the courtyard, and numerous pots of bay trees, shaped small and round, bordered the aisle. White silk bows had been tied to the backs of chairs, and Anna was grateful to Eleni for all the work she'd put into the wedding. Since the day she had brought the wedding dresses to the house, the two women had found a balance. Eleni was still formidable and not a woman to be crossed, but Anna had found respect there.

Anna hovered, alone, just out of view from the guests and the man who stood waiting at the top of the aisle. She felt an ache in her chest. There was no father to walk her down the aisle. No friends eagerly waiting to see her exchange rings, no family to witness her join herself to another person before guests, the priest, the sun and sky. She was so surprised to find *want* in her breast. The want that made her ache and tears press against the backs of her eyes. The want that made her wish so very much that she was doing this for love. That the man who would place his ring, his ownership, on her truly loved her. She had seen so many different versions of Dimitri over the last few weeks: the demanding, uncompromising man; the vengeful angel; the father to her child…the seducer, full of the dark promises he'd made her that night she'd agreed to be his wife.

She peered around the pillar that had been her protection until now, looking up at the large, sprawling family, all talking away and creating more noise than she could have expected for such a solemn event. Seated at the front, beside Eleni and her husband, was Flora with Amalia, happily babbling away with the older woman.

This was why she was marrying Dimitri. Not because of flowery words and promises she would neither have trusted, nor believed. Happy-ever-afters were for other people. Anna was making a life for her daughter, providing her and even her own mother with a security that she was simply not capable of by herself. This was what forced her to put one foot in front of the other as she began the long walk down the aisle to the man she would spend the rest of her life with.

As Dimitri saw Anna walk towards him, something stirred within his chest. She looked…alone. She had no one to walk with her, no one amongst the guests. Had he done that to her? Guilt poked and prodded painfully somewhere deep within him. She had no one to protect her…protect her from him. He had told himself time and time again why he was doing this, why *she* had forced him to do this.

But could he blame her? Her actions and decisions had been in defence of their child. Protecting her from a man who had been imprisoned, and was then said to have fathered a whole brood of illegitimates across the globe. Would he have not chosen to cut a person like that from his daughter's life? Within his own realisation, he could only hope that one day she too might understand what had brought them to the altar.

Now, seeing her make slow and steady progress towards him, he made a silent vow. The moment his ring was on her finger, she would be his to protect, just as he protected their daughter. The weight of that silent promise was heavier than anything he'd ever experienced. And for a moment he thought he'd felt it settle about his shoulders like a physical thing. Until he realised that it was Danyl, his best man, standing beside Antonio, his other best man, having thrown an arm about his shoulder.

'She is a thing of beauty, my friend.'

Yes, Dimitri acknowledged, she really was. The low neckline of the dress, exposing the deep tan of her skin, teased and hinted at a sensual promise that she had yet to offer him. The swirls of lace detail covering her chest and arms drew his gaze across her upper body, and the soft silk skirts kicked out each time she took a step closer to him. Desire pooled low in his stomach. The dress hugged every curve of her body, clinging tightly to her chest and arms, but the low neckline made his hand itch to slip beneath the fabric and feel the softness of her breast. She was the last woman he had touched, and she would now be the last woman he would ever touch. And he *would* touch her. He would have her. But *only* when she came to him.

The light caught on the tiny diamond earrings in her ears, making them sparkle in the setting sun. That was how he had imagined her during those dark days in prison, the light that pierced the darkness around him, the one memory he had clutched to him. If he had imagined her wearing a white dress, about to take his ring, he had purposefully removed the thought from his mind the day he'd thought she'd used him for money.

As she drew level with him he caught a momentary look of uncertainty, of doubt, but it was replaced with determination in a heartbeat. He knew the strength of will required to force away demons, and that called to him.

As the priest began, Anna turned to Dimitri, hoping that her eyes expressed the thanks she felt at the service being conducted in English. But as the words wrapped around her heart, she felt full of a kind of sadness rather than joy. Dimitri's voice rang with such sincerity as he promised to love her, to honour her above all else, and she wondered whether that could ever be true.

Lost amongst the words and her feelings, she almost missed the moment when the priest pronounced them man and wife. Dimitri turned then, giving her one last breath before his head lowered to hers and his lips claimed her for eternity.

The kiss was everything, overpowering and all-consuming. His lips unlocked hers, and the moment she felt his tongue against hers she was lost. Her arms came up around his neck of their own volition, clinging to him as if he were her only lifeline. Desire drenched her from head to foot as he brought her body against the hard muscles of his chest, pressing her breasts against his steel torso. She felt his thighs against hers, through the thin material of the silk skirts, and the evidence of his own desire pressed between her hips, shocking her, making her lose her breath to his mouth, the kiss, to him.

She was oblivious to everything but Dimitri…
until the first spattering of something hit her back
and caught in her hair. Then another wave of the
tiny little bullets pelted her arms and back again.
That was when she heard the cries from the guests
and looked up to find rice caught in Dimitri's thick,
dark curls.

'Did no one warn you?' he asked, his eyes seri-
ous, belying his playful tone.

For a second she thought 'no'. No one had warned
her about such a kiss. The kind that battered away
the walls around her heart, the kind that destroyed
her promises not to share his bed.

And then she realised he meant the rice. She'd
helped Flora, Eleni, Nella and many more female
family members fill hundreds of little bags full of
rice rather than confetti. She hadn't expected them
all to be used, but the rice was working its way under
the lace, catching in her hair as much as Dimitri's.
His dark, midnight-blue suit had little white dustings
from where the rice had been slung at him.

In a second she was caught up by the wave of
emotions coming from the guests—the joy and happiness was palpable on the air. Through the noise she
heard Amalia squealing with delight and turned to
see her scooping awkward fistfuls of rice and raining
them down on Flora's skirts. The laugh she couldn't
prevent fell from lips still bruised from Dimitri's
kiss, and she realised that she was still encased in
his arms.

'That's the first time I've heard you laugh since

that night three years ago, *agapi mou*,' he said for her ears only. The laughter subsided and she looked at him with sombre eyes, until another wave of rice hit them yet again, and Dimitri raised his arms about her as if to protect her from the onslaught. That one small action touched Anna more than she could ever have imagined, soothing some of the ache that lay in her heart.

The chaos from the dance area of the incredible hotel holding the reception was something to behold. Dimitri looked on as Antonio stood with his phone pressed to his ear, presumably whispering sweet nothings down the phone to his fiancée, who had been unable to make the trip. Danyl looked bored as he entertained yet another hopeful candidate for the position of his wife. The dark-haired woman beside him looked more interested in Dimitri's cousin than Danyl, he thought ruefully.

The place beside Dimitri at the head of the table was empty, his father having made his excuses to leave almost the moment dessert had been served. Anna was just bidding his stepmother a surprisingly fond farewell, Eleni's fingers brushing over the pearl bracelet Anna was wearing, a smile in his stepmother's eyes Dimitri had never seen before. Eleni caught his gaze just before she left, nodding at him in a way that poked at something in his chest.

All the guests seemed to be having a wonderful time. Flora was at her table with the now sleeping

Amalia resting against her shoulder. It reminded him that Anna had no one for her here and prompted his question to her.

'Would you have wanted your mother to be here? Or, your…?' He trailed off, realising how crass it was to bring up her father.

Anna turned to him as surprise was replaced by the heavy sigh that escaped her lips. 'My mother would have probably made a scene, and… I made my peace with my father's absence three years ago.'

He frowned at the timing, but her words provoked a different thought.

'Is that why you didn't try harder to tell me about Amalia?' He knew his angry words were wrong the moment they left his lips. Hurt slashed her cheeks pink.

'I thought we put all this behind us when I agreed to marry you. If not—'

'No. I'm sorry. I shouldn't have said that,' he admitted. 'Please, we were talking about your father…'

'The night we met, I had just come back from trying to find him.'

The woman he had met that night in Ireland had been… He'd thought she was resolved, absolutely sure of herself. Had he got it wrong? Had that night been one in which he'd seen what *he* wanted to see, rather than the truth? Had the woman he'd sought to exorcise his own demons been already shattered by those of her own? A woman defined by *his* needs rather than hers? He was almost afraid to find out.

'About three weeks before we met, I'd found some letters that were kept in the attic I was hoping to renovate for the bed and breakfast. All had been returned to the sender. Recognising my mother's handwriting, and the first name on the envelope, I realised the letters must have been written by my mother to my father.'

'Did you read any of them?'

Anna frowned, taking a sip of water from the glass in front of her before answering. 'I didn't feel that I could. These were my mother's letters. If they were full of hate and anger, I didn't *want* to read them. If they were full of love and need, I *couldn't* read them. But I had my father's full name and address. I used them to find that my father owned a small restaurant in London. It had recently won an award, which was why it was so easy to find.'

Her eyes had lost some of their sparkle, and she gazed over his shoulder as if seeing some imaginary scene.

'Without telling Ma, I booked myself a flight to London, using some of the savings my grandmother had left me—those Ma hadn't been able to drink away,' she explained sadly.

'It didn't go well?' Dimitri asked, pulling her back to the present.

'I went there believing that if he saw me there would be some kind of innate biological recognition. In my head, he would start to cry, embrace me, take me back to his home, perhaps even find a way to help me to help Ma.'

The pain in her voice as she expressed such simple hopes from her father cut through him like a knife. Anna looked out, seemingly unseeing of the guests, of the night sky that had descended to cover the deep sea beyond.

'He was busy. The restaurant was packed full of people, and the staff, clearly members of his family—his *new* family—were run off their feet. He glanced at me briefly, not really taking me in. Just trying to find somewhere out of the way to put a single diner. The ease he had with the people around me, his distraction… I didn't feel able to speak to him. I just… I sat where he directed me to sit and watched them together. Laughing, joking, shouting even, as someone got an order wrong from the kitchen. But I was on the outside looking in. I didn't even order any food. They'd forgotten about me in the busyness of the restaurant and I just… slipped away.

'By the time I got back to Ireland, my mother had convinced herself that I wasn't coming back and had drunk her way through most of the bar. That was why I was wearing her shirt the night you came to the bed and breakfast. I wasn't supposed to be working, but she was in such a state that I couldn't have let her anywhere near the guests. I'd just welcomed the last couple when you arrived on the doorstep. I nearly didn't let you in,' she added ruefully.

He looked at her, unable to voice the fear that he'd taken advantage of her that night, but he didn't have to. Yet again, she read his thoughts as if he'd said them out loud.

'Don't look at me like that. I knew what I was doing that night. It was reckless, and foolish, but I wanted it. You. That night, I wanted you.'

That night. Not now. But in that moment he could tell that they were both imagining what their lives might have been like had she not let him in. But Anna seemed to skip over the thought quickly.

'I feel so stupid for thinking that my father might have been able to recognise me on sight. I suppose that it's a childish fantasy,' she said, and because she'd turned her head away he nearly missed the question that fell from her lips. 'Is that how you felt when you first saw Amalia?'

Dimitri could tell that she was both hopeful and fearful of his answer. And he wasn't sure how to reply. Saying yes would acquit him in her eyes but would damn her father. And he couldn't bring himself to do such a thing on their wedding day.

But it was too late. She'd seen it in his eyes, he could tell.

'I'm pleased you had that. It's an incredible moment when you see your child, hold her for the first time, recognise that burst of love that tells you that you would do anything, *anything* to protect her. That your world has irrevocably changed and there is this little person in the centre of it all. That the purpose of your life is now them.'

'Do you understand, then,' he pressed on, 'why I did what I did? Why we needed to marry?'

'I understand it,' she admitted reluctantly. 'But I will never forgive you for doing it the way you did.'

* * *

The cool night air bit into her arms as the boat took them back from the hotel on the mainland to Dimitri's island home. Little lights marked the jetty for the boat and the wind loosened tendrils of hair about Anna's face, causing her to hold them back so she could see her footing.

Flora bid them goodnight, but she was still holding Amalia in her arms as she made her way back to her small home at the foot of the hills beneath the sprawling mansion that was to be their home.

'Where is Flora taking Amalia?' Anna asked Dimitri, a sense of dread pooling in her stomach.

'Back to hers for the night. All the bedding and things that Amalia will need was moved this morning.'

Fury cut through her. 'Without consulting me? You arranged for my daughter—'

'*Our* daughter,' he cut sternly into her sentence.

'To spend the night somewhere else, without my knowledge?'

He stopped in his tracks and turned back to her, standing steady on the wooden jetty, being gently rocked as the boat made its way back to the mainland shore. 'What outrages you more? That you weren't consulted on the whereabouts of your daughter, or that you no longer have a barrier to stop you from acting on your desires?'

His taunt was as cruel as it was accurate.

'Don't change the subject. You failed to consult

me on where our child would spend the night. You can't do that.'

'And how,' he said, running a hand over a face that suddenly seemed exhausted, 'do you think I felt, about all the decisions you kept from me?'

'But this is new for you!' she cried into the night. 'I've been doing everything on my own, every day, because you went to prison, because your assistant led me to believe that there were hordes of women out there like me.'

She gulped in a breath of cool air and that was all the time he needed to undo her completely.

'There is no one out there like you.'

'Because I'm the mother of your child?' she demanded, both terrified of and eager for his answer.

'No, not just that.'

For just a moment, he loomed over her in the darkness, blocking out the light of the moon until all she could see was him. All she could see was the desire in his eyes. And then he turned and left her standing on the jetty, watching his white shirt disappear over the crest of the hill that led to the house.

Damn him.

By the time she had summoned the courage to return to the house, she had realised the truth of his words. The courage she had needed was not for fear of him...but of herself. Of just how much she wanted to give in to her desire for Dimitri, to relish the pleasure she knew he could give her.

Dimitri was at the drinks cabinet, his tie hanging

loose at his neck, the glass of amber liquid nearly to his lips when he turned to look at her.

'Did you want one?' he bit out reluctantly.

'I don't.'

'Because of your mother?' he asked, curiosity ringing in his tone.

'Haven't we had enough of my personal life for one day? I'm going to bed. Alone,' she tossed at him over her shoulder.

'Not interested in consummating the marriage, then?'

'You've blackmailed me into wearing your ring. Now you want to blackmail me into your bed?' she demanded, turning back to him, still dancing around the edges of want, need and self-denial.

'I told you before, I wouldn't have to.'

'You're arrogant.'

'And you're stubborn,' he threw back at her.

His eyes locked with hers and she felt it, that thread of electricity that joined them, that cried to the world of their attraction.

'There you are, standing as if full of anger and righteousness. But it's neither of those things, Anna, is it?' he demanded. At his very words she felt the cords that tied her to those feelings begin to fray, slowly breaking, thread by thread. 'Inside, you're quivering with desire.' He took a step towards her, only increasing the tremors she felt break across her skin. 'Your pulse is racing, not with injustice, but need.' She tried to slow her breathing, but the flutter she felt at her pulse points was undeniable.

'Your cheeks are flushed, not with fury, but arousal. There,' he said, his fingers hovering above the lace that barely covered her breasts, 'your own body is straining towards me, desperate for my touch.'

She batted away his hand, but her heart wasn't in it.

He looked at her with assessing eyes, as if not quite understanding why she would fight this so much, why she would deny them both the pleasure they so desperately wanted.

'What are you so afraid of?' he asked.

It was the softness of his voice in the darkened room that undid her. That buried its way into her chest, lodging on the aching breath that shuddered from her lungs. If he'd been angry—if he'd shouted—she would have used it to fuel her indignation. But he hadn't. His words were like a verbal key, unlocking her soul and baring her to him.

In the deepest reaches of her heart, she knew what it was. She knew that she was terrified that she wouldn't just be giving her body to Dimitri, but more… Her heart.

But the words wouldn't come. Some innate sense of self-protection prevented her from revealing such a weakness. She looked up at him, swathed in the shadows of the room, marvelling at how the light from the moon cast him in silver finery, lighting the sharp angles of his face, making his dark eyes seem to almost glow. He was stunning, powerful… irresistible.

If she'd thought he'd turn away from her silence, she was wrong.

Instead, he pressed closer to her, crowding her, tempting her.

'Ask for what you want, Anna. It is your right.'

'As your wife?' she spat at him, desperate to cling to anything she could use to maintain the barriers she had put around her heart three years before, longer even. The barriers he was bashing through with the force of a storm.

'No. *Theos*,' he growled. 'As a *woman*.'

It was as if he had let loose a battle cry to everything feminine inside her, begging, pleading with her to reach for him, to take what she wanted. And it was so tempting in the darkness of the empty island home. What he was asking her. What he was telling her to demand from him. He was right—she had been using their daughter as an excuse, as a shield from the simmering tension that had always, *always* been there between them. It seemed like the simplest of things, but Anna felt the decision like a pendulum, swinging either way, weighed down, but pushing them forward to an undeniable conclusion.

Dimitri could feel her need, so strong he could almost taste it. He cursed himself to hell and back because by illuminating her desire for him he had served to increase his own. His arousal pressed hard against the dark linen trousers he had worn for the wedding.

Her eyes flared and he could see her wavering. He

could feel the struggle going on inside her, he could see it in her sea-green eyes. He'd promised her that *she* would beg—the irony was not lost on him. In that moment he would have given almost anything to have her succumb to him. In that moment, it was he who was poised on the brink of begging.

'You did that first night,' he reminded her. 'You demanded everything from me and I gave it willingly and I would not refuse you this, ever. So—' Dimitri took a step towards her '—you want me?' he demanded.

She looked almost mutinous, but finally said the word he'd been longing to hear. 'Yes.'

'Say it.'

'I want you.'

The thrumming that had unsettled the air about them stilled. She could still walk away. And he honestly couldn't have blamed her, but he saw her fingers hesitantly reached for the back of her dress. *Christe mou*, he was going to die if she had to undo all those buttons. He closed his eyes and heard the sound of a zip sliding down its fastener.

When he opened them again he watched the slow slide of the dress as it slipped, first from her shoulders, revealing her naked chest, the slopes of her breasts perfect as they rose and fell in time with her rapid breathing. She pressed the dress over her hips and it fell from her waist, pooling in a white silk puddle at her heeled feet.

Her chin rose defiantly as she stood there in nothing but her shoes and a white silk thong. He took her in all at once, the sight of her nearly undoing him completely. He felt the tremors of his own arousal begin to threaten his control.

'All of it. Take it off.' He gestured towards her thong. He watched her eyes widen a fraction. Good. It was good to see her as unsettled by this thing between them as he was. A masochistic part of him wanted her to stop. To refuse his last demand. Because if they took this step…there would be no going back. He would be making her his wife, in more than name only. And once he had what he wanted, he wouldn't let go.

Her thumbs slid down her hips and hooked under the thin lace of her underwear. Fire burned his lungs and Dimitri realised that he'd forgotten to breathe. This was what she did to him. As if she knew it, her hands hovered at her sides, waiting, taunting almost.

'Take. It. Off.'

His voice shredded the last of her uncertainty and he watched, heart in mouth, as she slid the flimsy material down over her hips, lifting long, lean, tanned legs, sweeping it down over her ankles, and she tossed it to the side.

'Say it,' he commanded.

'I've already told you… I—'

He shook his head slowly.

'You bastard.'

'That may be, but I still want you to say it.'

She started to tremble then—not with fear, no. Desire and want was clearly written in her gaze and satisfaction spread through him to see her as much at the mercy of their attraction as he. She bit her top lip as if to prevent her from saying the one thing he needed to hear. The one thing that would start what they had both wanted from the very first moment they had laid eyes on each other.

He wanted to take that lip within his own teeth. He wanted to lave it with his tongue, taste her cries as she found her pleasure in his arms. It was an all-consuming want that he wouldn't be rid of until he had her beneath him again.

He closed the gap between them with the last step he would take.

'Say it.'

Her white teeth loosened their grip on the plump pink lip.

'Please,' she whispered on a ragged breath.

He reached for her then, drawing her to him as his lips crashed down against hers, pressing her body entirely against his. Her lips opened to him, his tongue filling her mouth, meeting her own. *Christe mou*, he'd only once ever found this feeling before, only with her.

He lifted her from the pooled silk at her feet, drawing a gasp from her that he felt down to his soul. Her legs came up around his waist, his hands went down to the backs of her thighs, glorying in the soft skin he felt there, and he pulled her against him and she gasped again when she must have felt his desire.

Through the thin material of his trousers he could feel the heat of her; he wanted to touch her, taste her. His clothes were too much. He needed them gone.

He walked them up the stairs to his bedroom, the one she'd never been in. He kicked open the door and realised that someone had been in here since he'd left. He let her legs go, sliding her down the length of his body, and took in the rose petals scattered across his silk sheets, the tiny candles that had been placed around the edges of the room providing little star lights casting the barest of shadows.

He took it all in dispassionately because his sole focus was Anna. As he took one step forward she retreated, until her legs were pressed against the mattress of his bed. She nearly fell back, but he held her in place. Trembling. She trembled at his every touch.

She sat down on the mattress and he went to his knees before her, taking her calves in his hands as one by one he undid the little shoe straps around her ankles.

Her eyes never left his, locked together by wanton curiosity and need. Her hands balled the silk sheets of his bed in her fists as if to stop her reaching for him and Dimitri felt the cord of his desire for her tighten.

Her small fingers slowly reached up to the loosened tie, slipping the material away from the knot and sliding it slowly, torturously, from around his neck, tossing it aside just as she had done with her panties.

Her hands, hot, pressed against his chest, either side of the buttons, before turning their attention to releasing the small buttons from their holes. *Christe mou*, this was taking too long.

His own hands came up to either side of his shirt and he tore at the material, sending buttons flying, and cast the ruined garment from his torso.

Her eyes widened again in satisfaction as he stood, making quick work of his belt, sweeping off his trousers and briefs in one go. And he stood there, tall, naked, needing and wanting.

Anna felt her mouth dry the instant he stood above her, glorious and powerful, his bronzed skin glinting in the glow of the tiny lights that littered the room. It was dark enough to see his features, and the storm behind his unrelenting gaze. They stared at each other for an impossible moment, two gladiators about to do battle.

They moved together at the same time, Dimitri coming towards her, her moving up off the bed towards him. Their bodies crashed together, his powerful arms reaching around her, pulling her against him. The cry of pleasure falling from her lips as she felt the entire length of his naked body against her own was stopped only by his kiss.

His hands roamed over her body, the same way they had done three years before, touching, moulding, feeling every part of her. Her back, her thighs, her breasts. God, the things he was doing to her breasts. He leaned her back over his arm, his tongue playing with her hardened nipple, wringing another cry from her mouth, as his clever fingers taunted the other. And it wasn't enough. The need to feel him, inside her, was so utterly overwhelming.

'Dimitri...please.' The words came unbidden from her own mouth, her voice husky with a desire that she was almost ashamed of.

'What is it you want, *agapi mou*? How is it you'd like me to take you? To please you?'

The words caught in the back of her throat. She didn't know how to do this. How to express what it was that she wanted. She wanted...everything. She wanted him to touch her, she wanted him to taste her...she wanted to taste him. But the words wouldn't come.

As if he sensed her inability to speak, a small smile curved that sinful mouth and he pressed her back into the soft mattress, moving with her, allowing her to feel the weight of him against her, over her. He leaned on one arm, trailing his free hand across her neck, between her breasts, down over the stomach that had borne their child. As if the same thought had struck him, he bent to press kisses against the slight swell of a stomach that had been almost perfectly flat three years before. Was he taking in the changes that pregnancy and birth had wrought on her body? Did he find them distasteful? But his kisses soothed her fears, driving heat and sparkles of sensation across her skin. His hand continued further down her body, gently pressing her thighs apart. And then he found the heart of her.

Her hand flew to his, not knowing whether she was going to push him away or press him to her. It felt incredible, the pleasure he was wringing from her. She felt her back rise from the mattress, her chest eagerly reaching for his own. But instead of satisfying her desire he pulled back, raised himself to take her in. He took her hand in his other and pressed it over his as he continued to caress her intimately.

Gasps rained down from her lips as he thrust a long finger deep within her. One, then two, filling her, but it wasn't enough. His lips came down on hers as his tongue echoed the movements of his quick fingers. Her skin was alive, and her breath came in pants. Words, unspoken before, freed by the pleasure he was giving her, fell into the room. Begging words, pleading words she'd have had the sense to prevent if she were in control of her body, of her mind. But she wasn't.

The hard jut of him pressed against her stomach and she shifted her hips, wanting him, needing him inside her. She was so close to an orgasm, the little lights of the room turning into starbursts in the edges of her mind. But then he stopped, and her heart did too.

She had a moment of uncertainty, until he pressed her thighs further apart and plunged into her deeply in one swift motion, bringing her to completion, bringing her out of her mind. A small well of hysteria bubbled deep within her, and for a second Anna lost all sense of time, all sense of place, and only Dimitri remained, the feel of him as her muscles held him in place within her.

Just when Anna thought she'd found her breath, he started moving, slowly, languorously almost, but deeply, so deeply, she couldn't tell where she ended and he began.

Even three years before she hadn't felt anything this incredible, the power of him turning her helpless, and she gave herself over to him completely. Again and again he brought her to the brink of yet another orgasm, and just before she could fall he would slow the punishing rhythm, as if testing the very limits of his own control. Minutes gave over to sensation, time gave over to pleasure and only when she felt him harden even more did she find the truth of their joining. He stilled, biting his bottom lip as if preventing the same cries she'd given freely from escaping. She felt him shudder and release himself into her at the very same moment she fell into the abyss.

CHAPTER SEVEN

Dear Dimitri,
I wanted more. More than you were willing
to give.

THE SOUND OF Amalia's laughter woke Anna from her sleep. Her body ached in a way she'd only known once before and she stretched out beneath the sheets, loosening her muscles. She didn't have to open her eyes to know that Dimitri had left their bed. Had left the room. For a moment, her heart stuttered and she was back in her bed in Ireland three years before. Confused and disorientated. Only this time, she didn't run through the small bed and breakfast looking for him, wondering where the man she'd given her virginity to was. Wondering if he would ever come back. This time, Anna knew that—even though he had left her bed—he would be having breakfast with their daughter, as he had done every single day since they had arrived in Greece.

But it didn't mean that she was any less confused. Last night, Anna had asked him for what she wanted

and he had given it to her. Again and again throughout the night they had reached for each other. She had
given him the thing that he had told her she would:
her body. *But*, she lied to herself, *only her body*.

She came down the stairs and what she saw held
her back. Dimitri was holding Amalia in his arms,
gibbering away in a nonsensical mix of English and
made-up words that Dimitri pretended to understand
perfectly. Amalia thrust out a fist and grabbed hold
of Dimitri's dark hair, and instead of brushing her
aside he simply laughed.

Was this what she had kept her daughter from?
Not the pain and hurt she had promised herself over
and over again, but the love of her father? A small,
but very powerful, part of her wondered whether instead she had actually been protecting herself. The
sight was so striking, it took her a moment to see
that Dimitri was dressed in a suit, as if he were…

'You're going to work?' she couldn't help herself
from asking. 'The day after our wedding?'

Flora grumbled from the kitchen, as if understanding not the words, but the sentiment.

'The bank doesn't stop just because I got married,
Anna,' he said as if scolding a child. 'I have meetings to attend and a charity function to organise.'

Amalia, as if noting the change in tone around her,
started to fuss. He walked over to Anna and placed
Amalia into her arms.

'I'll be back, but most likely late, so don't wait
on dinner for me.'

With nothing else said, he left the house. The

sense of concern she'd felt earlier grew into a living, breathing animal in her chest. Now that she had given him what he wanted, was he going to retreat? Was this how their marriage was going to be? Shame and foolishness taunted her fragile heart.

It had taken Dimitri three sentences to cut through whatever fantasy she had clung to from the night before. It had taken less than thirty seconds for pain, sharp and acute, to slice through laughably thin armour, poking and prodding at old wounds.

Instantly she began to question what she'd done wrong, what she'd said to make him leave. The familiar pins and needles shivering across her skin, vibrating within her chest, reminded her of her childhood, when she would wait at the school gates for the imaginary figure of her father to come and get her. But he never had. Anna had promised herself that she'd not feel like this again. And she wouldn't. She slowly pulled each block of stone back into place around her heart, refusing to mistake sensual intimacy with emotional intimacy. She may have the security of wearing his wedding ring, but she knew from experience that a gold band didn't mean a thing.

Dimitri found himself pacing the length of his office yet again. Through the glass frontage he had watched as the sun set over the Athens's skyline, as he tried to focus on the numbers for the last financial quarter rather than the memories of losing himself in Anna's arms. Each of the seven days since their wedding had been the same. He would leave for work after breakfast with Amalia, the moment that Anna appeared from their bed. He wouldn't return home until the sun had long since set and would find Anna asleep on the sofa, or in a chair in the living room amidst a pile of second-hand English paperback books. He would pick her up and take her back to his room, where they would make love long into the early hours of the morning.

But they had barely exchanged a word. It was as if their life was playing out in silence. As if he was afraid of what he would reveal, or what she would ask of him: the one thing he didn't even know if he was capable of.

Dimitri could count the number of people he trusted on one hand. Antonio and Danyl were the closest thing he had to a family. His father had been cold and distant his entire life up until recently, and Dimitri still wasn't sure he could trust the changing tide of their relationship. But it was Anna who was threatening to undo him. Seeing Anna with Amalia, it hurt. Watching her prepare his daughter's food, watching her soothe away her tears, it reminded him of his mother. And all the memories he'd sought to suppress for years were coming to the surface.

Little things, like the way his mother had made the best, sweetest baklava—so big it resembled a loaf and had to be cut with a bread knife—the way that she had put a plaster over his knee when he had fallen. The way that, even after her long day at the restaurant, she would still find the energy to read to him at night. The feel of having her there, the comfort and the love that she had wrapped around him, protecting him from the bad things of the world. Protecting him from his father's absence and rejection.

And those were the memories he didn't mind so much. But it was what came after that shook him to his soul. The shock, the pain when all of that was taken away in a heartbeat. When the policeman had stood in the hallway to their apartment asking the seven-year-old Dimitri if he had any other family. It was the weeks, the months that followed—that was what he didn't want to remember.

At the age of seven he'd made himself an island, realising that no one else could protect him. And that was the very reason why the charity event he was holding with the other members of the Winners' Circle in Kavala tomorrow night was so important.

Returning to the island, early for once, he felt fresh from the boat trip that had blown away the dark thoughts of his day. He hovered in the hallway to the kitchen, steeling himself against the childish giggles of his daughter and Anna's laughing response, and he wondered if he would ever get used to the sounds of such domesticity. Whether he even deserved them.

The moment Anna saw him, she cut him an almost accusatory look.

'You're back,' she stated with an undertone he couldn't quite decipher.

'Yes, it is my home,' he stated before being able to stop the defensive tone from creeping into his voice. He tried not to wince at her hurt reaction. When did his own home become such a minefield? He bit down against the flare of irritation. 'We are travelling to Kavala tomorrow.'

'Are you?' Anna replied, purposefully misunderstanding him, Dimitri was sure.

'*We* are attending a charity gala dinner there.'

Flora swooped in, prepared to clear the field for the battle she had realised was to come. Amalia went willingly into her arms and Flora retreated outside to the garden.

'I'm sure you will have a wonderful time.'

'Anna,' he bit out.

'Dimitri,' she returned.

He cursed. This could go on all night.

'I'm not going,' she repeated.

He searched her tone for a hint of anger, or defiance, but was surprised to find there was none. Just a simple statement of fact.

'You have to be there.'

'Why? Why do you want me there?'

Such a loaded question. One he wasn't yet prepared to search his soul to answer. 'The press will be there. And it's expected that you—as my wife— will be too.'

Anna felt her stomach clench and she instinctively pressed a hand to soothe it. So it wasn't because he actually wanted her there. No. It was for appearances' sake. She could feel the ridges and tension almost vibrating from her forehead. Why was it that everything Dimitri did or said seemed to continually feed into years-old insecurities?

For a whole week she'd said nothing, betrayed none of her feelings, terrified of making this strange stalemate situation worse. These briefly exchanged words were the most they'd said to each other since the morning after the wedding.

'If that is the only reason you would like me there, then I'm afraid I shall have to decline.'

'Have to... Anna, I'm not joking about this. You are coming with me.'

'Until you give me a good enough reason, I'd rather spend that time with our daughter.'

She'd thought he'd stalk out. Leave. Yet again. But there was something anchoring him to the spot. And for just a moment she glimpsed a side of Dimitri she hadn't been privy to yet. Gone was the amused, indignant man, gone was the patronising husband. He stalked towards her in just a few long strides, towering over her with broad shoulders that blocked out the setting sun, his eyes as dark as the night promised to be. The demand she had laid at his feet loosening the bonds around his secrets.

'You want to know? Fine. I didn't go straight from my mother's home to my father's.'

It took a moment for Anna to orientate her mind to how that might fit in with the charity event, but Dimitri pressed on while she struggled to keep up.

'As I said before, it took my mother's sister two months to track down my father. But during that time, I was put into the care system. My mother's sister couldn't take me in—she lived nearly five hundred kilometres from Piraeus in Kastoria. Her work wouldn't allow her to take more than a few days away, and she couldn't afford to lose her job.

'So it was decided that I should be put into the care system, until something suitable could be arranged. What I didn't know at the time was that the "something suitable" was code for until my father could be persuaded to take me in.

'The people managing the unit were kind, or as kind as they could afford to be. The first day, my jacket was taken—and trust me, my mother wasn't rich, so it wasn't expensive by any standards. But, when I did nothing, my shoes were taken the next day. It's funny what you cling to as a child. Amalia has her sculpture, I had only clothes—small things that my mother had worked hard for and were my only reminders of her. Pieces of her were being taken away from me, bit by bit, and I did nothing to stop it from happening.

'Each day, I asked the adults what was happening, where I would be going, when I would be going. And each day they said, come back tomorrow.

'Two months is a lifetime for a seven-year-old boy. Friendships made, fights lost… Most of the boys had grown up on the streets, tough, mean, clever. There was one kid who tried every day to run away, desperate to go back to where he'd been. But that wasn't an option for me. There was nowhere for me to go back to.'

Dimitri took in a breath. It shuddered in his chest,

as if the memories were shaking him to his very core. There had been no protection then. No Danyl or Antonio—the friends he wouldn't meet until university. At the time, his seven-year-old self had thought that he was numb. Numb with grief, numb to the chaos and tension that he'd lived and breathed…but it had scarred him deeply. And only now, forcing himself to recall this time, did he realise how close to prison it had been. How they had both been tinged with the same fear, the same raw vulnerability. His life had not been his own, in either situation. And both times had forced him to realise that there was no one out there who could protect him. He had to protect himself.

'I soon learned that if I didn't fight back, if I let that soft heart form friendships with unworthy people, people who would lie, steal and cheat their way through the care system, I wouldn't survive.'

He let out a huff. 'I know that sounds dramatic, I know I would have continued to live, breathe, be fed. But…the boy my mother raised? Not so much. So I became tough. I fought for what little belongings I had, fought to keep the things that reminded me of her. I promised myself that I would never be in that situation ever again.'

I promised myself that I'd never let anyone be my weakness again, his inner voice concluded. Until Manos. Until that one thread of hope had formed and been severed.

'When my father finally took me in, I had the best that money could buy—education, clothes, the biggest house I'd ever seen. It didn't matter that Manos hated me on sight, that my father barely spared a thought to me other than how he could turn me into an asset for the Kyriakou Bank. It didn't matter my father's wife watched me like a hawk, as if I'd do something eventually to hurt her child. It only mattered that they gave me access to the tools that would allow me to ensure I was never beholden to another. I worked hard at school, at university in New York.'

The memories of meeting Antonio and Danyl softened features he hadn't realised had become rock-hard.

'And the moment I had enough money, enough power to create a charity for homeless children, I did. Antonio and Danyl helped too. Because none of us ever wanted a child to feel that same sense of helplessness, that same uncertainty. So once a year there we hold a gala. This year it is in Kavala, and we—you and I—*will* be there.'

Dimitri refused to turn to Anna. Refused to see the pity he knew would be there in her eyes. He'd never wanted her to look at him in that way. He *never* wanted to see that from her.

'Why didn't you just tell me how important this was, and *ask* me to come with you?'

Unbidden, the words that came surprised even himself. 'I didn't want to risk that you'd say no.'

He felt her small hand reach his elbow and gently pull him about to face her.

'You have to trust me, Dimitri. If I knew how important this was, then of course I would come with you. But trust works both ways, Dimitri. You can't demand truth and fidelity from me, and not give it in return. So if there is something that I don't want to do or, in fact, *do* want, then you have to trust me too.'

But, in the darkest reaches of his heart, he knew that this was what he was most afraid of.

Anna shifted uncomfortably in the back of the limousine taking them to the gala at the exclusive hotel in Kavala, the same limousine that would pick them up at the end of the night and return them to his apartment nearby.

Had it only been last night that Dimitri had opened himself up to her? She felt as if years had passed. She was beginning to see through the mask that Dimitri wore to the child, the vulnerable boy who'd been lost and needed, *deserved*, kindness. Beneath his words she'd felt his pain, and was finally beginning to understand his need to secure certain things for their daughter. She'd once so easily dismissed his notion that something might happen to her, or to him. For her it was hypothetical. For him it had been real. A lesson hard learned.

She felt that they'd made a step forward last night. That slowly they were forging connections she both longed for and feared. But she also knew that he was holding something back. Because he was speaking of a childhood pain, not the pain of the present that she could see hovering around him like an aura.

Flora and Amalia had stayed back at the island, neither Dimitri nor Anna willing to upset Amalia's routine for just one night. A few hours ago, Amalia had played with diamonds and pearls as if they were plastic bricks, Anna's heart lurching as she saw her daughter's chubby fist gripping enough jewels to support them for a lifetime. The same expensive jewels that now hung around her neck like a noose.

The cool silks of a turquoise dress skittered over her skin like a caress—one that she hadn't received from Dimitri since their conversation the night before. She had marvelled at how the beautiful colour had sat against her sun-darkened skin. Never before had she seen the colour of her skin as anything other than something that marked her as different, that reminded her constantly of her father's absence from her life. But here, in Greece, it came to life; *she* came to life. *Stunning* was how Dimitri had described her one night. *Beautiful*, another, and more recently *his*. But the night-time words were left in the dark, and the day…?

She had darkened her eyelashes with liner and mascara, accentuating features she now wanted to own, to shine as if both her appearance and her emotional scars had made her who she was today. She'd dusted the lids of her eyes with a golden shadow, bringing the vivid green of her irises to light. Was it Dimitri's confession, his struggles with his past, that had helped her find her own strength? The fact that this incredible, powerful man, with his own dark secrets, could be proud and confident? *If only he had chosen her for herself…*the unwelcome secret voice of her heart whispered.

Brushing that thought aside, and focusing on an inner sense of confidence, she proudly walked up the red carpet that lined the steps to the incredible hotel built within an old imaret in the port town halfway between Thessaloniki and Istanbul. As they passed through the high, sweeping archways she ignored the flash of the press's cameras, the questions called out to Dimitri. She followed his actions, smiled when he smiled and, when he turned to her and claimed her lips with his own, shock momentarily gave way to desire, inflaming hopes of what might come after the gala.

The moment they entered the gilded ballroom, sound hit her like a wave, a thousand voices in a hundred languages echoing off the stone walls and marble floors, but all hushed in an instant, turning to greet Dimitri like a long-lost friend. After the fourth introduction, Anna stopped trying to remember people's names, instead taking it all in and falling back into warm greetings she was well versed in from her experience at the bed and breakfast.

When Dimitri guided her towards yet another group of people she felt herself smile as she recognised the man that stood in the centre of a tightly knit group. The sheikh who had been at their wedding, the royal she had been almost too scared to speak to, now greeted her with warmth the moment his eyes lit on hers.

'Dimitri, so kind of you to join us,' said the heavily accented voice with mock reproach.

'I knew that this evening would be doing well in your more than capable hands, Danyl.'

'Anna, lovely to see you again,' Danyl said, by-passing Dimitri's compliment.

The lack of formality between her husband and the prince drew only the slightest of frowns from the two dignitaries, who made excuses and left the small group. Anna's eyes were drawn to the cool beauty pressing herself against the sheikh. In Anna's mind, she was exquisite. Ice-blonde hair, perfectly swept back, as if ready and waiting for a crown, topped a face with the palest of skin. Milk and honey was the first thing that came to Anna's mind.

'Allow me to introduce Birgitta Svenska,' Danyl said without making eye contact with the woman, his tone as bland as if he were reading off a restaurant menu. Anna thought she saw a brief flash of hurt in Birgitta's features.

'A pleasure,' the woman said in cultured tones that betrayed no hint of a Scandinavian accent. Her gaze remained cool and assessing, until she took in Anna's husband. Calculation turned to appraisal, and Anna was surprised by the fierce streak of posses-siveness that ran across her shoulders.

'Any sign of Antonio?' asked Dimitri as if he too had somehow passed over the European beauty.

'He couldn't make it. He sends his apologies. Emma's morning sickness has kept her in their apartment in New York.'

Anna smiled. 'You should tell her to try ginger tea. It certainly worked for me.'

Dimitri turned to her. 'You had morning sickness?'

'Yes, Dimitri. Oddly enough, it's actually quite common,' she replied, gently mocking him. Though her tone had clearly done nothing to assuage the sting reflected in his gaze.

'I hadn't expected her to be experiencing it so soon. He only just called to tell me the news,' he said, turning back to the Sheikh of Ter'harn. 'Anything new from Australia?' Dimitri asked.

'Nothing you cannot find out for yourself, Dimitri.' It was then that Anna was reminded of the sheikh's true power, the look in his eyes enough to quell an army. Her husband responded only with a raised eyebrow.

'She is fine,' Danyl reluctantly admitted.

'She?' Anna couldn't help querying.

'It has been the talk of the racing world,' scolded Birgitta, as if somehow Anna's ignorance was a fatal flaw. 'The Winners' Circle syndicate is trying the impossible with a female jockey. Three wins on the Hanley Cup hasn't been achieved since...'

'Mason's father,' concluded Danyl.

Birgitta eyed her companion with speculative eyes before enquiring after the Kyriakou Bank's recent success, effectively shutting the sheikh and Anna out from the conversation. Danyl's only reaction was an amused quirk of his lips, before turning his powerful attention to Anna.

'How is your daughter?'

'Well, thank you. She's thriving in Greece.'

'As are you, it would seem.'

Anna smiled at the compliment, letting it warm her, but she still couldn't help but glance at the intimate way Birgitta was conversing with her husband.

'Don't worry, Anna. He only has eyes for you.'

Anna cocked her head to one side, considering his words. Before she could contradict his statement, Danyl pressed on.

'I have never seen him with any woman the way he is with you. And it is good. As it should be. I cannot say that he's the easiest of men.'

'No. He's not.'

'But he is very much worth it. Once his loyalty is earned, it is steadfast. As is mine. So should you need anything, Anna, *anything*, just say.'

The sincerity in his tone touched her. It made her happy that Dimitri had people like Danyl in his life, after the loneliness of his childhood. And now, it seemed, perhaps she did too.

Birgitta politely excused herself from the conversation with Dimitri and disappeared. In an instant, Danyl's whole demeanour changed. He ran a hand over exhausted eyes.

'Another potential bride?' queried Dimitri.

'She certainly seems to think so. I feel like a prize bull.'

Anna felt a smile lift the corners of her mouth at the easy admittance of the powerful royal before her, but quietly retreated from the personal tenor of the conversation.

Dimitri watched Anna slip away into the crowds, dark intent swirling in his stomach. The first time he had laid his eyes on her that evening, clothed in the gentlest of turquoise silk, he had wanted to order her back into the room, strip her of her dress and lock her in. The only thing that had stopped him was the shock of his own caveman-like reaction.

'You seem tense. Certainly more tense than usual,' Danyl remarked.

'It's… We're staying at the apartment here tonight.'

'And you haven't been back since Manos's arrest.'

'No,' Dimitri replied, casting his eyes around for a drink, for anything to distract him from the direction of this conversation.

'Perhaps it is a good thing that Anna is with you.'

'I think it may be *because* Anna is with me.'

'She's a good woman, Dimitri.'

'She's not just a woman. She's the mother of my child.'

'Is that all? You have the look of a man in more than lust, Dimitri.'

'You know me better than that, Danyl.'

'But does Anna?'

Anna came from the bathroom stall out into a beautiful, Ottoman-styled bathroom. Large mirrors adorned high arched walls covered in exquisitely detailed tiles in shades of blue and white. As women bustled around the room she was almost surprised not to see them in period dress.

As she washed her hands she caught sight of Birgitta at the basin beside her.

'So you are Dimitri Kyriakou's new bride.' The statement was accompanied by such a deep study, Anna wondered if Birgitta was trying to understand why Dimitri had chosen her.

'Yes, I suppose that would be me. Unless he has another one squirrelled away that I don't know about.'

With a slight inclination of a perfectly smooth shoulder, Birgitta sidestepped Anna's attempt at humour. 'Though I wouldn't expect it of Kyriakou, there are certainly some men out there I wouldn't put it past.'

Anna honestly couldn't tell if Birgitta was being funny or not. 'You mean Danyl?'

An arched eyebrow reminded Anna that she was speaking of royalty on a far too familiar basis.

'If the Sheikh of Ter'harn were married, I doubt very much that I would be here.'

With no trace of self-pity in her tone, Anna couldn't help but marvel at the woman's apparent stoicism.

'Oh, don't look at me like that,' Birgitta continued in a weary tone. 'I know what my role is here tonight. *Danyl*,' she said, 'needs a bride. My family need me to make a good marriage.' Another shrug of her beautiful shoulder punctuated her concluding statement. 'We—wives or *potential* wives—are nothing more than conveniences and possessions. We make of it what we will. And don't misunderstand me—I will make the most of this.' The determination in Birgitta's tone made Anna reassess the woman in an instant. She only hoped that Danyl knew what he was getting into.

But her words had struck a chord within Anna. She certainly hadn't been a convenience for Dimitri, she knew that much. But the determination, the idea that she could make something of this, rather than sit passively by and let things happen to her... Hadn't that been what Dimitri had said to her the night of their wedding? That she needed to ask for what she wanted?

Was she so terrified, she thought sadly, that she had truly stopped asking for things for herself, for her future? Was she so convinced that she would be rejected, or left, abandoned, that she had stopped even *thinking* of her future, of herself?

As she re-entered the ballroom she located Dimitri easily amongst the throngs of people. The breadth of his strong shoulders drew her to his innate power. As if sensing her, he turned, his eyes finding her in a heartbeat. The hairs on Anna's arms rose, goosebumps raining down over her skin at the sensual promise of his gaze.

She wasn't willing to allow this marriage to simply happen to her. If she wanted to make their marriage work, then she couldn't live in fear, or hold herself back. She needed to have faith in both her husband and herself, faith that he wouldn't leave her and faith that she was good enough to make him stay. And, with that thought ringing in her ears, she took a glass of champagne from the nearest waiter, taking a deep drink and allowing the bubbles to explode in her throat, sparking excitement and something like hope deep within her.

CHAPTER EIGHT

Dear Dimitri,
Today I found you. The real you.

DIMITRI HAD DELIVERED the keynote speech about the poverty that was affecting Greece's families, the orphanages that were filled not just with orphans, but also with children with loving parents who had turned them over to the state because they simply couldn't care for them whilst holding down the myriad jobs they needed to take to keep a roof over their heads. He'd highlighted the plight of just a few small families, giving voice to the crisis that affected so many, and he'd felt righteousness ring in his voice—a righteousness that he so rarely felt about his own business these days, aside from the need to compensate for Manos's awful actions.

He'd tried to avoid thoughts of his half-brother's betrayal for so long, but now that the limousine pulled up to the apartment he hadn't stepped foot in for over three years, he wondered if Anna could sense the dark thoughts that were descending upon him. One look at Anna, who had shifted in her seat to look up at the large building towering over the port's skyline, the silks of her skirt rising up against perfect thighs, and Dimitri struck down the well of arousal firing within him, instead focusing on Danyl's insightful question.

No, he thought. Anna didn't understand his difficult feelings about love, didn't understand how it had been routed out of him by his father's aloofness and his mother's death. Didn't understand how it had been impossible for him to let a woman get close to him. How impossible it still was. He cursed himself, thinking that he should tell her. Warn her. But the words wouldn't come.

'This is yours?' she asked, awe evident in her tone. From any other woman, he'd find it jarring, a leading question that instantly became calculating. But no matter how much he searched her voice, he couldn't accredit Anna with that.

'Yes,' he bit out gruffly into the night as he escorted her from the car.

He entered the foyer, pulling out the key card for the lift access to the penthouse apartment, feeling rather than seeing Anna follow on his heels. Mirrors lined the lift, rose-gold lighting turning Anna's skin an even more delectable shade. Standing so close, he could smell her perfume in the air, warmed by her body. His hands itched inexplicably, desperate to reach out. As if she sensed that need somehow, she leaned ever so slightly towards him and for a moment he fought against the desire to step back, to create some kind of distance…the distance that was with them before he'd taunted her on their wedding night. Before he'd laid a challenge, a demand, at her feet.

He should have let her have her paper marriage, because ever since that moment, his brain had seemed to stop functioning and instead he was immersed in feelings, wants and needs he'd been able to prevent for years.

The doors to the lift opened up directly onto the foyer of the apartment.

Dimitri didn't know what he'd expected. Owing to his brother's use of it, he'd somehow imagined the walls to be painted black…evidence of drugs and prostitution perhaps—the things that he had bought with other people's money. Perhaps broken TVs and plates from one of Manos's legendary tantrums.

Anna swept past him, deeper into the apartment.

'This is lovely,' she said, looking around the open-plan kitchen and living room. And it was. It didn't have any incredible floor-to-ceiling windows wrapping around the apartment, but the balcony leading from the master suite could be seen through the windows of the living room.

But, despite the incredible view, it wasn't enough. It didn't feel open enough. The walls were beginning to press down on him, as if his whole being was shaken with the need for air, for the open sky. Memories of his time in the care system, of the small, bunk-bed unit in the prison, each thought scratched against him like barbs, drawing thin lines of blood invisible to the eye.

He needed a drink. He needed his bed. His bed, alone. Not with her. Not with the wife whose very presence was taunting him—the woman whose image he had clung to as if his sanity depended on it as he had lain in prison listening to the sounds of the other prisoners, hundreds of men all breathing the same air. He needed to stop all these chaotic thoughts.

He didn't realise that he'd been pacing the room until he felt Anna's gentle hand on his forearm, stopping him almost midstride.

'What's wrong?' she asked, concern easy to read in her eyes.

'Go to bed, Anna,' he ordered, hating that his own words sounded so harsh.

'No,' she said, cocking her head to one side as she looked at him, as if she was trying to understand a puzzle.

'I need you to leave.'

'I'm not going anywhere.'

The growl that emerged from lips thinned by anger and something else Anna couldn't quite identify should have been chilling, but instead it fired her own determination to understand her husband. She could see the pain, the fury emanating from him. So, instead of turning and fleeing, she stepped towards Dimitri's potent frame, relished the powerful vibrations coming off him in waves, allowed them to fill her, to imbibe her with that same sense of energy and power.

'What is it?' she demanded.

The indecision in his eyes tore at her heart. If he couldn't trust her, then what would that mean for their marriage? Because that was what she had begun to think of it as. Not just some blackmail scheme to access his daughter…but a partnership. But if she couldn't get Dimitri to see that, she didn't know how much longer they'd be able to go on.

'It's… Ever since…'

Anna was shocked. She'd never seen her husband speechless before, grasping for words. Even in his fury he was eloquent and impossible.

'It's okay,' she assured him, closing the distance between them, placing her hand on his arm—the muscles beneath her palm locked tight.

'It's not okay. None of it's okay, Anna.' He spun out of her hold and left her standing in the living room. But she wasn't going to let him get away that easily. She followed him through the side door—ignoring the palatial master suite—and out onto the balcony, where Dimitri was now standing, fingers gripping the balustrade, the white of his knuckles clashing with the stone.

'You're not going to let this go, are you?' he demanded.

'No.'

Dimitri turned to see her standing, strands of her dark hair caught on the gentle breeze, proud, immovable, determined. She had changed. It was as if after their wedding night she had taken something within her, inside her, keeping her strong, making her fearless. Or perhaps she had always been that way, and he had only just seen it now.

If he were any kind of man he would match her strength, and that was enough of a thought to loosen the words that had clogged his throat in the living room, that had stuttered to a stop before escaping.

'I don't like being in enclosed spaces. It's too much like being in prison.' He looked at Anna, this woman who wanted more from him, demanded more from him…but just how much he was willing to give he wasn't sure any more. 'White-collar crime. That's what they call it in America.'

'Why did you go to prison there and not in Greece?'

'The clients Manos chose to steal from were American, and he did it through the American branch. He believed that the Greeks had lost too much already. It was, apparently, the only altruistic thought he'd ever had—but don't for one second take him as a Robin Hood figure. He couldn't have been more of a cliché if he'd tried, using the money to fund his drug addiction, prostitution, a lifestyle even more lavish than this,' he said, gesturing to his stunning apartment.

He was surprised when Anna came to stand beside him, desperate to cling to the warmth of her body heat, allowing it to warm him as his words, memories, turned him cold.

'You were in prison for fourteen months,' she said, more of a prompt than a query.

'Between being released on bail and the court

case, I spent a total of four hundred and twenty-seven days in prison.'

'But you were innocent.' Her outrage was a pale echo of the one he had nursed for what felt like years now.

'Yes, but so was every single man in there.' Her frown drew a grim smile from his lips. 'It's what they all said.'

'But for you it was true.'

'I remember the first time the lead investigator's questions changed. They had enough evidence to convict me, but I had two very good witnesses for one occasion when it was simply impossible for me to have taken the money.' An unspoken question rang loud out into the open air. 'No, Anna, not bedfellows. Antonio and Danyl. Even the FBI couldn't argue with the Sheikh of Ter'harn.'

'So why didn't they let you go?' Anna demanded.

'They needed time; they would need me to follow the court case through, until they had enough proof to bring down the real perpetrator. The Americans take financial crime very seriously and they didn't want to risk him escaping their justice again.'

Anna took all this in with wide-eyed shock. If he hadn't experienced the whole sorry mess himself, he could almost have felt sorry for her.

'What did you do, while you were in there?'

At first nothing came to his mind, a blank wall protecting him from that time. Initially he'd thought his innocence would protect him. Not from the other prisoners, but from his own mind. 'Not much, is the answer to that question. I read.' He shrugged as if it were nothing, as if he hadn't spent hours, days, climbing the walls…nursing a secret fear that he'd never get out, that the FBI had lied to him. That he'd spend the rest of his days there. 'It's funny what your mind will do to you when you have no control over your day, your time. I spent time in the gym, trying to work off some of the energy that I suddenly had. And when I couldn't escape my body, I escaped into my mind. I… I thought about you,' he finally admitted. Hours and hours, losing himself in that night they'd had together. Holding the memory of her as a beacon against the darkness that had sometimes seemed to overwhelm him.

'What did you think about me?' Anna was almost too scared to ask.

'I could show you if you want,' he taunted, the gleam turning his eyes darker than burned caramel. But she refused to let him distract her.

'Later perhaps,' she replied, softening the rejection with a smile. She knew there was more. It wasn't just that this proud, powerful man had been caged like an animal. She sensed, somehow, that it wasn't the imprisonment that had really hurt. She needed to go deeper, poke deeper; *he* needed her to.

'And when you got out?'

The taunt dropped from his eyes, his gaze once again out to the silent night sky, whilst inside a storm raged within him.

'Everything was both the same and different. I had initially fooled myself into thinking that it had been some high-level executive stealing from the company. My father had promised that he would provide the FBI with all the help they needed, and when the FBI first came to tell me they had identified the criminal I was relieved. I was actually fool enough to think that my father and brother had saved me. That all the time during my childhood, when I felt on the outside looking in, when I felt…when I was made to feel like an imposition, like an imposter…it all disappeared. For just a moment, I felt that I had family and that they had put aside their feelings and somehow found proof that had saved me from imprisonment. I felt love for them, the tendrils of connection… And when the FBI revealed that it was Manos I was struck dumb.' It was as if an axe had come down on the roots of his foundations.

Even though Anna had known the outcome, that it had been Manos's betrayal that had put him in prison, she felt the echo of his first moment of shock cut through her like a knife.

'I had been betrayed by a man who shared my blood. Not just betrayed, for that implies some kind of implicit wrongdoing on my part. He actively laid paperwork that set me up.'

She could see the pain of that hurt, she knew that pain, had borne it every day with her mother. But Dimitri's actions, although poorly motivated, had enabled her mother to find the help she so very much needed. And now Anna wondered if she could help Dimitri heal some of that pain, those hurts…that betrayal.

'Ma's drinking…it was hard. Each time she would promise to stop, and I would go through the stages of grief, denial, anger. Each time it was harder and harder to forgive, because each time it felt like a greater betrayal. Each time it *was* a betrayal. But it seems that the rehab centre is working for her. She'll be coming out soon and she's really trying this time. And I want to thank you for that. I wouldn't have been able to provide her with that kind of help.'

He was watching her, wary. She had to tread lightly and feared that, even if she did, he could see what she was coming around to. He was like a panther, sleek, powerful, ready for fight or flight.

'And that's why this time it's important for me to be able to forgive. Her drinking is a disease. It's not something she can help; it's not a choice.'

He turned away from her, back to the skyline of Kavala.

'Manos had a choice. It wasn't a disease. He chose to steal money, chose to set me up.'

Pressing down the hurt she'd felt as he turned away from her, she once more placed a hand on his arm. 'I could imagine that your brother might have felt inadequate next to you. Clearly your childhood with your father was difficult…but is it the same now?'

Dimitri frowned. 'He's been…different, recently,' he reluctantly acknowledged.

'Relationships aren't static things, always staying one particular way. If there is hope for you and your father, could there be hope for you and Manos? I'm not saying that Manos is nice or even worth your sympathy—not at all. But sometimes when some-one acts unnecessarily horribly towards another per-son, it's not about that other person, but about them. Which means that he might be at least worth your understanding.'

Anna's heart was in her mouth. She hoped, so much, that her words were getting through to him. Because he carried too much. He held too much within him, bottled up. It needed to be released if they were ever to have a chance.

Her chest ached and she resisted the urge to rub away the pain. But it wasn't the same kind of pain that hurt and lashed out. It was the kind of ache that grew and grew until it overshadowed everything. It was huge and terrifying, because in that moment she realised that she loved him.

The Dimitri who had spent one wild night with her in Ireland. The Dimitri who had been wrong-fully imprisoned and so much more damaged by his half-brother's betrayal… The Dimitri who had forced her into marriage, and the one who had also opened her eyes to her own strength, her own de-sires and needs. The Dimitri who, she realised, had never really known comfort and understand-ing from the very people he should have first re-ceived it from.

This time, she allowed her body to take over. Casting all thought aside, she let her heart guide her hands and her actions. She wanted, *needed*, to show him as much as she could that she did love him, that she could and would give him that comfort, that support. She might not yet be able to put it into words, and even had she been able to she wasn't sure that Dimitri was ready to hear them, but this... she could do.

She took his hands, still clenched around the balustrade, in her own, gently releasing the iron grip he had on the stone. She pressed his palms against the bare skin beneath the V of the silk folds of the dress, allowing him to feel the beat of her heart. She reached up to him, to his jaw, relishing the feel of the stubble shadowing the harsh lines of his face.

Dark eyes, full of suspicion and surprise, watched her every move.

'Anna—'

'I don't want to go to bed, Dimitri.'

'I don't want this, Anna.'

'Do you want me to tell you what *you're* feeling? What *your* body is saying to me? Is it *my* turn, Dimitri?'

The sense of her own arousal gave a strength to her words that surprised her. She allowed it to fill her, to empower her. He shook his head again, but this time he didn't speak. She closed the distance between them. She felt rightness settle around her, making her movements sure.

She started with his tie, the crack of the silk as she snapped it away from his neck and threw it to the ground the only sound accompanying their harsh breaths. She pushed the black silk jacket from his shoulders, revelling in the feel of the superfine white shirt covering his powerful chest, the muscles there a solid wall.

She slid buttons through holes all the way down, slipping aside the shirt and glorying in the feel of his flesh beneath her palms. Was this how he had felt on their wedding night? Powerful and conquering? How had she gone all these years without this feeling? How had she allowed herself to become so afraid of her own desires?

Her hands went to the buckle on his trousers and were immediately halted by Dimitri's.

'Be careful, *monadiki mou*. Once you start this...'

'I have no intention of stopping,' she whispered into his ear, pressing her chest against his. She pulled back and barely had the chance to prepare herself for the bruising kiss that crashed down on her lips.

Their tongues warred for dominance, for control, but this time Anna was determined not to back down. Not to give over control to Dimitri. She pushed him back against the stone balcony, lifting the silk skirts of her dress over one thigh as she anchored her knee around his hip, pressing her core, the heart of her, against him, relishing in the hard length of his arousal. She shifted, moving their centres until she could almost feel him, through his trousers, through the silk of her dress, just where she wanted him, needed him, to be.

Dimitri's guttural curse escaped their kiss and his hands came around the curves of her hips, dragging her even further against him. Their groans mingled, just before he pulled away.

'You're killing me, Anna.' His dark eyes gleamed in the night. 'You're tearing me apart.'

Before Anna could say that he was putting her together again, that he was healing over the cracks in her heart, he took the silk straps of her dress and tore the material from her body, exposing sensitive flesh to the cool night air.

Her bare breasts heaved against his chest, his hand diving to the thin scraps of lace of her panties, his expert fingers finding the heat of her, pleasuring her, torturing her as she shifted in his embrace. It was as if he was trying to wring those same emotions from her with his seduction, tearing at her very being. His other hand had come down on the top of her thigh, anchoring it beside him, refusing to let her retreat, keeping her open to him, to his expert manipulation of her body.

It was an exquisite torture, but it wasn't enough. She wanted to give him this, for her, for him, for them. She needed to.

She let go of the grip she had on his neck with one hand, trailing her fingers down his chest, catching on the dusting of dark swirls covering his torso, letting it guide her hand further down to beneath his trousers. She relished the feel of his hardened length, wrapping her hands around the base of him, glorying in the flare she saw in his eyes, the moment of indecision she read there. Her breath caught in her throat while she waited. Would he push her away? Would he allow *her* to pleasure *him*?

The back of Anna's hand brushed against the

back of his, and their eyes locked in an instant. She told herself not to look away, refusing to close her eyes against the pleasure she was giving him as she stroked up and down, the way his bronze eyes darkened, the way a deep flush rose to his cheeks. Briefly she wondered what it was that Dimitri saw, how she looked, but as his long, lean finger plunged deep into her a gasp fell from her lips and she felt his satisfaction vibrate from his very soul. He thought he'd won this game of wills, this wicked contest of seduction. But he had severely underestimated her.

Using his distraction against him, she pulled away and, bending before him, still clad in her high heels and thong, she took him into her mouth. She let a smile play at her lips as curses littered the air, some in English, some in Greek… She didn't care. She felt empowered by his reaction. From the periphery, she could see his hands gripping the stone balcony, she could feel how his powerful, muscular thighs trembled, his hips beginning to shift beneath her.

'Anna…' His voice was practically a growl.

Reluctantly she let him go, but that didn't mean she was ready to let him take the lead. She drew herself up the length of his body slowly, stepping out of the reach of his arms. She watched as he kicked his trousers away from his legs, stepping out of them, fully naked. She took him in, powerful, proud, unashamed of his nakedness beneath the stars, open to the elements. With any other man, she imagined it would make them vulnerable, but with Dimitri it made him glorious.

'What game are you playing?' he demanded.

'No game. No playing. This is real and this is me, and what I want,' she said, knowing the words to be truer than any others she'd spoken to him.

A rush of emotion hit Dimitri's chest hard. In all the different moments that he'd seen her, he'd never seen Anna like this. The closest to it was the night that they had spent together three years before, the night they'd conceived their child. But here, Anna was incredible. The woman that would have hidden from him, would have needed him to draw her out of herself, to put words to the desire and attraction she felt, was now owning it, not asking for something she was afraid of, but demanding it for herself.

His own nakedness didn't shame him, it never had, and now he wanted Anna's. And if Anna thought that her lacy thong protected her in some way…she was wrong. An errant thought ran into his mind, the same way it had done on their wedding day… *Who would protect her from him?*

She took a step back towards him, having only moments ago retreated from his reach. She took his large hand in her smaller one, flattened the fist he had unknowingly made it into and returned it once again to the centre of her chest, the flat plane in between the two perfect mounds of her breasts.

She pressed his rough palm against her smooth, silky skin and Dimitri forced his body under control. He wouldn't allow the shakes that had racked his body the moment her mouth had found him to happen again. The sight of her, before him, on her knees, had almost undone him.

But he could tell, now, from her eyes, from her tone, that this was something she craved—no, needed. An undercurrent of change was shifting beneath the surface of her skin, and he was drawn to it, fascinated by it and unable to take his eyes away from her.

He brought a hand up to her cheek, unable to resist the need to trace his fingers across her skin, his hand cupped her jaw, and once again he dipped the fingers of his other hand beneath her panties and into the seductive wet heat between her legs. *Christe mou*, she was so ready for him.

He spun her in his arms, bringing her back against his chest, her bottom cradled between his hips. His fingers stroked her, wringing cries from her mouth and tremors from her body. The heat of her body, flush with his, stoked the flames of desire that licked every inch of his skin.

Never before had she come so alive in his arms, never before had she unleashed the control she held about her like armour. She was stripped of everything and relishing it. It fired his blood, settling deep within him. The sound of her breath, pants littering the air about them, came quicker and more urgently, her pleas flung into the night, begging and wanting, the very thing he had taunted her with before now serving only to increase his own need, his own arousal.

He pressed his finger, one first then a second,

deep within her and she cried out, reaching her own completion, falling forward and catching herself on the stone balcony. He held her body as she shuddered, each time her core gently tightening around his fingers.

It wasn't enough. It would never be enough. Now it was his turn, now it was what *he* needed.

He pressed his hands between the backs of her thighs, spreading her open to him, catching his curse before it could be let loose. She was incredible. He ran his hands over the curves of her backside, dipping his hands between her legs, casting his thumb out to catch the overly sensitised flesh and revelling in the way it sent a jolt through Anna's body, as she reached out to hold on to the stone balustrade.

He plunged deeply into her until there was nowhere left to go, and failed utterly to prevent the feral growl he unleashed into the air about them. The feel of his skin inside her, the easy glide as he slowly withdrew almost completely, before thrusting back again, quick, hard, deep. It still wasn't enough. As if sensing it too, she spread her legs wider, leaning back into him until she rested against his own thighs.

He thrust into her again, and again, never tiring of the feeling he was chasing, never tiring of the need to bring them together to an explosive completion. Once again, he drew his hand over her perfect breast, feeling the weight of it against his palm, moulding it, his fingers playing with her hardened nipple, forgoing the pleasure of taking it into his mouth, utterly overwhelmed with the intense passion her body was giving him. He dipped his fingers into the dark curls at the apex of her thighs, his thumb smoothing over her once again.

Her hot, fevered hand reached for his hip, grasping, pulling him into her more deeply, as if she was driven as much by this insanity as he. He wanted her to feel what he was feeling, that same sense of madness that was consuming them, that same sense of what they had become. It was exquisite torture as he pushed them almost to the brink, forcing himself to keep them there, hovering on the edge of the infinite nothingness of their own completion.

All about them, heavy on the air, their cries rang out into open air, the sound of his skin striking against hers the most intensely arousing thing he'd ever heard. All those nights in prison, never had he imagined the truth of their coming together, never had he been able to taste the strength of need, almost choking him now as he pushed them closer and closer to the edge.

That was his last thought, before his final thrust pushed them into oblivion.

Whether moments, seconds or hours had passed before his presence of mind came back, Dimitri couldn't have said. Anna was cradled in his embrace, all strength in her body lost. Picking her up in his arms, he walked them through to the bedroom, passing the bed and continuing on into the bathroom. Still with her in his arms, he walked into the large, glass-fronted shower and turned the handle, waiting for the water to become hot before he put her down on unsteady legs.

The intensity of their lovemaking seemed to have robbed them both of words. He poured gel into his hands, pressing it into her skin, her muscles, soothing away the aches he imagined she might have, over her breasts, between her legs, down her thighs. When she did the same for him, Dimitri pulled her back into him, desperate to once more claim that same completion.

He turned the shower off, covered her with a towel and dried them both before leading her to the bed. The entire time her eyes had watched him, his hands, his actions with an intensity that scared him. Something between them had shifted tonight, and he wasn't sure what that meant. Wasn't sure he even wanted to look too closely at it.

Just before sleep could claim him, Anna asked a question that surprised him. She wanted a honeymoon. Not to go anywhere, but just some time with him and Amalia alone on the island. Without Flora, without work… And, just before he fell into a deep sleep, he was pretty sure that he agreed.

CHAPTER NINE

Dear Dimitri,
I never guessed. I could never have imagined
it could be like this.

DIMITRI KNEW INSTINCTIVELY that he'd made a terrible mistake. Whether it was three days ago when he'd agreed to Anna's request for a honeymoon, or three minutes ago when he'd gone to war with his demanding daughter over breakfast. He had spectacularly underestimated the calming influence Flora had on Amalia. Spectacularly. The heat from the night before had been stifling and Amalia had woken up pitching to throw a fit. He empathised.

For the first time in months, years almost, he had nothing to do, or at least nothing he was familiar with. This 'honeymoon' idea of Anna's had exiled him from his business, business that had taken him two days to wrap up. His father had been almost gleeful to be rid of his brooding, obsessive need to pull their company back from the brink of the destruction Manos had caused. Encouraging him to enjoy his honeymoon, his wife and his daughter, his father had almost smiled as he had bid him farewell. Dimitri shook his head at the memory—wondering at the new tentative bonds of their relationship, amazed at the way it had begun to soothe some of the past hurts.

Had he really been that punishing at work? He cast his mind back over the months since he had come out of prison, all the days merging into one: fraught meetings with the board, impossible targets reached, devastated clients soothed and brought back into the fold—and all of which was done at an adrenaline-pounding pace. The trip to the Buenos Aires horse race last month and then one to Dublin, the only time away that Dimitri had allowed himself.

And he'd liked it like that, because it had kept him from thinking…from focusing on Manos's betrayal. But since the night in Kavala, since the night he'd opened up to Anna, shared some of his past, and his pain, he'd felt…lighter. And that scared him. Because he was simply not used to it. Since the age of seven, he'd been solely reliant on himself. And now he was beginning to trust the bonds that had been woven between him and Anna. But what scared him the most was that Anna had been right.

The moment that she had suggested speaking with his half-brother, a sense of ease opened up in his chest—his chest that had been in a vice-like grip ever since Manos was charged with the fraud and cover-up. Perhaps it was because for the first time he didn't feel as if he was facing his brother alone—that he had Anna and Amalia to return to, to share some of the burden with. Having Anna's support…it was different to the kind offered by Danyl and Antonio. It was healing. And he only hoped that he could do the same for her.

He turned from the kitchen table when Amalia cried out loud, forgetting the cup of coffee he carried. The searing heat as the hot liquid spilled from the rim of his cup drew a loud curse from his mouth.

Anna chose that exact moment to come into the kitchen and in once glance seemed to take in both his burned hand and furious mood, along with her daughter's loud, plaintive, dry-eyed crying.

'Can you do something about that?' he demanded roughly, distracted by the burn and thrusting his hand under the cold-water tap. He caught her raised eyebrow and instantly realised his mistake.

'Did you just call my daughter "that"? Really?' she demanded.

'Come on, Anna, I didn't mean it like that and you know it.' To his own ears he sounded exasperated.

'One of you in a mood I can handle, but both you *and* Amalia? Too much. As you have gone to such extreme lengths to "claim" your child, as you so artfully put it, this is what it's like, Dimitri. This was why I wanted a honeymoon. You wanted a wife and child—here we are. And now, I think, it's your turn to find out what parenting is truly about. Not just the happy breakfast times, but the hard times, when there's no reason other than our daughter's own demanding personality—one that I can only imagine she inherited from you—for her to throw a tantrum.'

'Did you even take a breath during that nice little speech?'

'Did you even think to ask what Amalia liked for breakfast?'

That stopped him in his tracks. 'What do you mean?'

'Figure it out, Dimitri. I'm going for a swim.'

Dimitri felt the anger and helplessness rise within him. 'You can't just leave me.'

'Yes, I can. There's nothing stopping you from being a father—you're perfectly capable of seeing to her food, her health and her safety. Now you need to learn how to do the hard stuff.'

Dimitri watched, horrified, as Anna stalked out of the house and down to the beach with a towel tucked under her arm and her head held high. He cast another look at Amalia, who by this point had stopped crying, as if she was as shocked as he that she would be left with him.

He left the counter and approached his daughter with caution. Each eyeing the other with deep suspicion, Dimitri stepped closer to the table where she sat in the high chair. He had watched Flora every morning, presenting Amalia with that same breakfast. He was sure that he'd done everything the same way that she had. He leaned forward to the little pot of prepared breakfast Flora had left him in the fridge with a label on it, but the label had been smudged. He dipped his little finger into the grey goo and tasted it, pulling a face as the paste hit his tongue. *Theos*, that was awful. What had Flora been thinking?

He reached for a glass of water to drown out the foul taste, and locked eyes with his daughter.

'Okay, Amalia, I defer to your better judgement. That was vile. Now, what else is there around here that you might like?'

As Anna made her way back up from the beach she was wondering if she'd made a terrible mistake. She'd wanted this time to just be a family unit without Flora, to prove to Dimitri, to prove to herself that they could make this work. That she had been right to trust Dimitri with her heart.

But what if she'd left her daughter with him and he'd failed? Her footsteps gathered speed, and by the time she reached the crest of the hill on which the house stood her heart was in her mouth and she was half terrified at what she might find.

But it was her daughter's laughter and infectious giggles that she heard first. Then the splash of water and, to her greatest surprise, a deeply voiced laugh. It stopped her in her tracks. She'd never heard Dimitri laugh. And for a second that was almost one of the saddest thoughts she'd ever had.

As she reached the flattened area of garden she saw Dimitri and Amalia in the infinity pool. He was holding her above his head, Amalia with her arms encased in little float bands, laughing hysterically as he swooped her in and out of the water. And suddenly she felt guilty for doubting him.

She walked back into the house to change and couldn't help the smile that formed upon the sight of the kitchen. Half-eaten fruit, breads and pastries littered the surfaces as if some grand eating competition had happened in her absence.

By the time she had showered, was dressed and leaving the room that had become solely used for her clothes, she heard Dimitri settling Amalia down in the living room to play. This time it was Anna who hovered in the doorway as Dimitri's gentle tones were soothing his daughter's excitement and redirecting her attention to the small building blocks she loved so much. It wouldn't be long before Amalia grew out of such easy distraction. It wouldn't be long before she was off to playgroup and then school. And for a moment her vision of the future jarred, because it had always been in Ireland that she had imagined those things to happen. But now the location had shifted to Greece.

Dimitri looked up and found Anna standing in the doorway, her usually open expression unreadable.

'I think Flora might have set me up.'

'I think Flora might have been teaching you a lesson.'

'You knew?' he demanded.

'I guessed,' Anna said with a shrug of her delicate shoulder and the faintest trace of a smile playing at her mouth.

'And you didn't think to warn me?' he replied, his tone readily losing the heat of anger and instead becoming filled with the warmth of humour.

'You're big enough and ugly enough to handle it,' she assured him.

As she passed him he reached for her hips and drew her towards him, leaning over her to crowd her, teasing her as she tried to bend out of his reach.

'You think I'm ugly?' he said, his head cocked to the side, the entire length of his body flush with hers.

'Hideous. Terrible. A monster,' she said as he punctuated her taunts with a kiss upon her neck. This Dimitri? This teasing, playful, impossibly sexy man? Simply irresistible.

'I am *not* a monster,' he mock growled as he pulled her into a kiss. A kiss that wasn't a punishment, wasn't demanding, but giving, generous and spine-tingling.

She met his growl with a groan of pleasure but batted him away and went to the fridge to prepare a snack.

'What time did you want to leave for Piraeus?'

'Forget it. We can cancel. Let's just go to bed. It's nearly dark anyway.'

'Dark? Dimitri, it's eleven in the morning!'

'No, Anna, did you not hear that? It was the nightingale, not the lark.'

Anna let out a gasp. 'How dare you corrupt Shakespeare to your own ends?'

Dimitri shrugged a nonchalant shoulder. 'If it would help my cause I'd—'

Anna cut him off with a kiss. His megawatt charm was more devastating than any of his previous anger or righteous indignation. The look in his eyes made her hope, dared her to believe that this was how things could be. And for the first time in three years Anna desperately wanted to throw caution to the wind, to seize this day, this moment, this feeling for herself.

Dimitri's phone pinged twice, alerting him to new emails, and he swept it up quickly and checked. If there was something secretive about it, the look of surprise, then of satisfaction, that flashed in his eyes smoothed over any misgivings. He looked…happy. That was what it was. For the first time since she'd met him…he seemed happy. And she couldn't help but feel that she had contributed somehow, she had helped him reach that state.

'Something important?'

'Two somethings, but I'll explain later,' he assured her, his eyes sparkling. 'Now, we have to get going,' he said, whisking Anna and Amalia up in a whirlwind of excitement and happiness.

Five hours later and Dimitri was worried. It had been an almost perfect day. They'd taken the boat into Piraeus and his car had picked them up and whisked them off to Athens, to galleries and the Parthenon. He'd laughed at Anna's sheer delight at a simple lunch of souvlaki, washed down with an ice-cold beer. The easy way she had with both Amalia and him was touching him deeply after the past few months fraught with tension and pent-up frustration. But his plans for his surprise for Anna were now complete, and for the first time he was beginning to doubt his decisions.

He'd wanted to give her something, anything, to

help show her that she had given him such a gift. Just
before they'd left for Athens, David had emailed to
say that Manos had agreed to his visit request. He'd
shared that information with Anna in the restaurant,
and the smile she had greeted the news with had only
inflamed the hope in his heart. It had felt right that
he should receive that news today—when his plans
for Anna had been underway in his home.

It had been a big project, and Dimitri had paid
handsomely to have the changes to his home made
and completed in just a few hours. He worried that
he'd missed something, forgotten something that
Anna might need. But he knew that wasn't what really concerned him. The greatest worry was that he'd
got it horribly wrong. That the surprise might not
quite be something that Anna would welcome. And
that fear? It was almost as great as the one he'd felt
about her not agreeing to their marriage.

'Are you okay?' Anna asked as the boat docked
at the jetty. The sun was readily setting and Amalia was tired, wriggling in her arms, after such an
exciting day.

'*Nai*. Let's…let's put Amalia to bed, and then…
then we can…'

Why was he finding it so hard to get out a simple sentence?

'Then we can…?'

'Have the rest of the evening to ourselves,' he
concluded, not having to fake the desire he felt at
the idea of having Anna all to himself. Spending
time with Amalia was incredible, but he'd missed

three years of Anna too and now he just couldn't get enough of her.

Instead of leading them into the living room, Dimitri led Anna, still carrying Amalia, straight up to the bedroom. If she went anywhere else, if she even turned on the lights, then the surprise would be blown.

When Anna went towards her room he nearly shouted for her to stop. She turned back at him, laughing.

'Really, Dimitri. What on earth is going on?'

'I...'

How had she made him so tongue-tied? Was it her or was it what he so desperately wanted to show her? he wondered.

'Come with me?' he asked, the uncertainty in his voice making him cringe inwardly. He wanted so badly to do something for her. To show her all the things that he seemed incapable of saying.

He took her by the hand and led her back downstairs. The sunset bled through the windows, lighting the living room and door to the study in orange hues. He paused outside the room that was once his study, marvelling at how easy the decision had been to give up his space in his home, once he'd given it up in his heart.

His hand paused on the door handle. For just a moment he took a breath. Looking back to Anna, he could see the beginnings of concern in her gaze. He shook his head; he didn't want her to be worried. He pushed open the door and stepped back for her to see.

For a moment Anna was too distracted by Dimitri, by the hesitancy written across his powerful features, to look into the room. But, following his gaze, she turned to look at what had once been an office and was now…

Speechless, she took a tentative step into what was now, from just a glance, an incredible art studio. The desk and computer had been removed and in their place were long wooden benches lining two walls. On the third wall was a stack of shelves full of huge, plastic-wrapped slabs of clay, and so many different-coloured glazes she didn't know where to begin. Her fingers reached out to touch the spindle of chicken wire she could use as a frame, rasps and rifflers, wire-end modelling tools, cutting tools and some she didn't even know the names of.

She stepped further in and saw the pottery wheel in the middle of the room, cast in shadow from the setting sun, through the huge French windows leading out to the patio, where she saw…

'Is that a kiln?' she nearly cried. 'You installed a kiln?'

'Is it the wrong kind? I didn't know—'

His words were cut off by a fierce kiss that ended all too quickly as Anna darted around the room, looking at all the bits and pieces Dimitri had somehow amassed in the last five hours.

'This is incredible!' she exclaimed on a sigh. 'But what happened to your office?'

'I moved it. To the room that you were in,' he said, not meeting her gaze, as if afraid of her reaction. 'I thought... I wanted you to be with me in my room, *our* room.'

Anna didn't know where to start, what to think, to say.

She was utterly speechless. She knew that things had been better between them since Kavala, but this? This was more than she could have imagined. Already her fingers itched to rip open the packets of clay, to pour over the different-coloured glazes and...the kiln?

She turned to Dimitri, her cheeks almost aching from the smile and wonder she felt. 'What did I do to deserve this?'

'You... I wanted to give you something that had been taken away from you. I wanted you to know that you can still reach for your dreams, that you can still have them. That Amalia, your desires and I aren't mutually exclusive.'

It was then that the cracks in the armour around her heart shattered completely. She rushed to him and pulled him into a kiss that hopefully expressed all the things she was unable to say. Her hands reached for his neck, drawing him to her, moulding his shoulders with her fingers, desperate for more, for that last little bit of him that was just out of reach.

She pulled back, sensing the uncertainty there.

'Do you like it? Is it okay?' he asked, his voice gravelly.

'It's perfect. It's amazing,' she said, looking about

her. 'You didn't have to get *everything*,' she said with a little laugh.

'I didn't want to miss anything.'

His words nudged at her. Nudged at a memory from when he had first found her and Amalia. Of just how much he had missed of Amalia's first years. And she wondered whether perhaps he might finally be ready to read the letters she had written to him over the years. Because finally, here, standing before her in a room he had created just for her, was the man she had always dreamed of. The real Dimitri.

'You didn't,' she assured him. 'You didn't miss a single thing. But there is just one thing left for me to see.'

He frowned his question to her.

'My new room,' she said, smiling, pulling him back into a deep kiss.

CHAPTER TEN

Dear Dimitri,
How could you do it? How could you break
my heart?

SHE DIDN'T KNOW how to speak to Dimitri, the Dimitri she married. So instead Anna wrote to the man who was the father of her child. The man she'd been writing to since the day her daughter was born. The man of her imagination.

But for the first time since she'd started writing the letters it was hard, almost impossible, to put pen to paper. For the man of her imagination was blurring into the man she loved, with his faults, his anger, his pain, but also the love she could see he felt for their daughter, the love that she had hoped he might feel for her.

A week ago he'd flown to America to see his half-brother. It was supposed to be for only two days, but he'd emailed her to explain that he'd extended his stay. She'd tried to tell herself that she was imagining the distance that had sprung up between them.

That what she was feeling was just a relic of long-ago hurts.

The last two weeks before that, the incredible time they'd spent together since that day in Athens, had been...like a dream. Anna couldn't remember laughing so much, loving so much. The Dimitri she'd seen had been playful, charming and utterly devastating. So she clung to that dream, rather than her fears. She clung to the image of the three of them, united as a family, and poured it into the first sculpture she'd made in nearly four years.

Every night since Dimitri had left she'd come to her studio after putting Amalia down for bed, and moulded, shaped and smoothed out her dreams and hopes for the future. She hadn't known quite what it was she was making—her fingers moving instinctively over the cold clay until it warmed beneath her hands—until after nearly six days she'd finally stepped back and seen what she'd created.

It was the sister of the first clay piece Dimitri had seen, all those weeks ago when they'd first arrived in Greece. Only this one was different. Instead of two orbs, there were three, all joined by a sweeping arc, binding the figures together, encasing them in an embrace. Her hope. Her family.

'It's happening now.'

Dimitri slammed the phone down in his office. He had to get himself under control. But ever since the night he'd visited Manos... He clamped down on those feelings. He couldn't allow them to jeopardise what he was about to do. For once, he was actually fearful of his own self, of the sheer fury that coursed through his veins. He feared that it was too much for him to control.

He was afraid that whatever twisted kind of love he felt for his father that could remain after what his half-brother had told him would make him weak. And would make him unable to do what he had to do.

He waited until almost all the staff in the office had left, before stalking down the empty corridor of the offices to his father's suite. He didn't want anyone else dragged into this mess. Before he entered his father's room, he looked back down the opulent halls of the empire of his family. He almost let go of a guttural sarcastic laugh that was threatening to escape from his tightly pressed lips.

These people weren't his family. They may have given him blood, paid for his education, but that didn't make them family. To think that he had actually believed his father, hoping for a fresh start, hoping for the connection he'd wanted almost his entire life. No. The only people he could rely on were himself and his true brothers, Antonio and Danyl. He had called them last night, explaining everything. They had offered him whatever he needed. But they couldn't help him with this. No. He was alone.

A small, Anna-sounding voice echoed in his mind. *What about me?*

And he shoved it away with all the force he could muster.

Dimitri pushed his way into his father's office,

closing the door behind him. He took in his father, a man who had grown to almost monstrous proportions in the last few days. So it was with surprise that he took in the wizened features of the man who had given his blood to him. Looking at him now, Dimitri saw a small old man who deserved neither kindness nor forgiveness.

'Did we have an appointment? You know I have a meeting with the shareholders to prepare for.'

His father was yet to look at him. Did he know? Did he know why Dimitri had come here today?

'It can't wait.'

With a frown, Agapetos Kyriakou lifted his head to finally look at his son.

'What is it?'

'I went to see Manos last week.' His father should have played poker. Nothing in his face betrayed fear, not even a twitch at the mention of his sons sharing a conversation. No. He was too good for that. Dimitri pressed on. 'I went because I wanted to find some kind of resolution with my brother. The same kind I had thought I'd found with you. I wanted to see if there was something, anything there of a relationship I could salvage. Imagine my surprise at what Manos revealed to me.'

Agapetos's eyes narrowed, suspicion clearly painted across his features. Dimitri needed his confession, not just to reveal his crime that it was *he*, not Manos, who had laid evidence leading to Dimitri, but because he needed to hear it from his father.

'I just want to know why.'

'Why what?'

'Why you did it.'

'Did what? Dimitri, I don't know what you're talking about. You seem a little unsettled. Perhaps you should go back to Anna.'

'That's the last time you ever say her name.' Dimitri's fury was ice-cold. It raised goosebumps on his own skin and he clenched his hands into fists, balled at his sides. 'Do not ever speak of her or my child again. Because you'll never see them. You'll never get to infect them with your lies or your bitterness.'

Instead of seeing his fury reflected in Agapetos's eyes, Dimitri was cut short by the sight of tears. As if all the fight, the power, the vitriol had fled from his father's body.

'So he told you.'

'Yes, he told me. I thought you had done absolutely everything you could possibly do to me. I thought that nothing you could do would surprise me any more—but I was wrong. And what *really* gets to me is that I should have known. Of course my brother wasn't capable of laying down a paper trail that led to me. He was barely capable of getting up in the morning.'

Dimitri didn't know how, but he was now standing right in front of the desk, towering over his father, who was shrinking back in his chair and almost shaking.

'I didn't have a choice,' he said, tremors racking his voice. 'My son is weak,' he continued helplessly. 'He could never have survived a prison sentence—

I don't think he will even now. But you?' he said, looking up at Dimitri. 'You are your mother's son. Strong, fierce and capable. The only way I could save one son was to sacrifice the other. I had to cover up Manos's theft, I had to lead them to you because no one else had access to the top-tier accounts. I tried, Dimitri. I just couldn't allow that soft, weak boy to languish in prison.'

'But why offer your olive branch at the party?' Dimitri demanded, giving vent to his deepest pain, the greatest betrayal. 'How could you even stomach to do it, knowing what you had done? Was it because you wanted to make up for your actions, or because you were afraid that I would keep digging, that I would uncover your involvement?'

Agapetos was almost sobbing. Tears ran down creases in his cheeks; red eyes, the irises bright blue, peered up at him. Seeking what—forgiveness?

'You want me to believe that you did this out of some kind of familial love? That you were trying to protect him? That it was some form of altruism?'

'Yes.' The need, the desperation in his father's tone could have swayed him. It could have saved his relationship with his father, his brother... It could have but for one ultimate truth. And that truth nearly undid Dimitri.

'But you loved neither of us enough to sacrifice yourself.'

The hitch in his father's breath was enough for Dimitri to know how right he'd been, the glint of selfishness in the man's watery eyes all the confirmation he'd ever need.

Dimitri had thought he'd feel powerful, he thought he'd feel as if he'd righted some incredible wrong. But instead, all he felt was empty, exhausted and devastatingly betrayed. So much more so having let himself hope…hope for a future, a relationship with his father, the kind he'd always wanted, no matter how badly treated or ignored. This was the death knell on that hope, and it made him feel like the vulnerable seven-year-old he'd never wanted to be again.

He left his father, tear-stained and miserable, in his office. Dimitri didn't even stop to collect his bag from his own office. For all he knew, his computer was still on.

The silence of the lift grated on his frayed nerves. His shirt scratched against his chest, and he wanted to escape. He left the foyer of the offices and crossed the street with powerful strides, fury making his steps long. He approached the unmarked blue van and pounded on the back doors.

They swung open as Dimitri reached inside his shirt and pulled the wire from beneath the cotton, ripping away the small pieces of tape securing the tiny microphone from its moorings.

'You got what you need?' he demanded of the FBI agents who had heard everything. His father's confession, his family's dirty laundry…the pain.

The man in the windbreaker nodded, and Dimitri stepped back as agents poured out of the van and entered the offices of the Kyriakou Bank, ready to arrest his father.

Dimitri turned and walked away as he heard one of the men ask about him giving his statement.

'Not now,' he shouted over his shoulder and stormed deeper into the city.

Dimitri's feet were sore. Not just aching but bruised and battered, since the handmade Italian leather shoes were unable to withstand the furious pounding as he had walked through Athens down to Piraeus. His heart felt cold, the way it had done when he'd heard of his mother's death. Was he grieving again? His confrontation with his father certainly felt like grief. It scratched at him, ate at his skin, his bones. Dimitri's mind was full of anger and pain, and he pounded the pavement the way that the rain had battered his home less than a week before.

The streets had changed in the last few years. Graffiti marked buildings that had once seemed magnificent. Posters with anti-austerity jargon were clumsily pasted over advertising for expensive clothing, anger vibrating up from the very foundations of Greece. Poverty had spewed out people into the corners of streets and back alleys, each face peering out of the gloom showing the darkest of circumstances. It matched him, matched his mood. No one dared approach him, such was the sheet of armour his fury and pain had created.

If the private-boat captain thought anything strange about his appearance nine hours after dropping him off that morning, he said nothing. They surfed the sea in silence as the sleek motorboat cut through the waves between the harbour and his island, the mindless hum of the engine providing a constant grinding drone that churned his thoughts.

For the first time in years Dimitri felt the plush, leather-lined seats, the chrome and steel of the boat an outrageous luxury, jarring against his humble origins with his mother. Was this how Anna had felt? Pulled from her quiet, small life, and thrust into his obscenely rich world?

When had he become immune to it? To the money and lavish lifestyle? A lifestyle that his brother and father had been so desperate to protect at all costs. It had taken two years for the Kyriakou Bank to survive the last scandal. What would it take to ride this one out? And for the first time in years, Dimitri wondered if he shouldn't just let it all burn to hell. But somewhere in him remained the last threads of his pride, and the determination to succeed that had seared his soul was clamouring to get out.

He stalked into the kitchen, where Flora and Anna were talking. Flora took one look at him, scooped up Amalia and disappeared.

And there stood Anna. A vision in white, the pristine sundress so pure, so innocent, he almost couldn't look at it, at her. All he knew was that he needed to protect her and Amalia from what was about to happen. Protect them in the way that his father—his family—had never done for him.

And in that moment a small, terrible part of him

blamed Anna. Blamed her for lifting the lid on this greater betrayal. Blamed Anna for making him think that he was better off with her and his daughter in his life, when all along he should have known. Should have trusted the knowledge and the simple fact that he was better off alone.

'I have arranged for you to return to Ireland.'

'What?' Her shock was so sincere, so confused, it hurt. Hurt a part of him that he had thought long since gone from his father's machinations.

'Your mother is due to leave the facility in the next few days. It would be good for you to be there when she does.'

'What's going on... What happened?'

What happened? The question cut through him, and he wanted to scream, *Everything. Everything happened.*

'My father has been arrested.'

Anna started across the kitchen, coming towards him, comfort, sorrow, confusion, all warring within her gaze. He held up a hand to ward her off. He couldn't do this if she touched him. He had known what would need to be done, and his father had been only the first step. But this second step was the only way he could protect Anna and their daughter.

'There is going to be a huge scandal. Bigger than any that have come before. The press will be camped out on my doorstep, and it will be nasty.'

My doorstep, not *ours.* That was the moment Anna realised Dimitri was truly sending her and their daughter away. Her head was spinning. She had been trying to tell herself that she'd imagined his withdrawal, but she hadn't. Clearly she hadn't.

'I don't care,' she replied, clinging to her love for him, to the tentative bonds they'd formed before he'd gone to see his brother, before…this. 'I don't care if the hounds of hell come after you. I'm staying. *We're* staying,' she said, desperate to remind him that it wasn't just her he was getting rid of, but their daughter too. 'This is the worst of *for better or worse*. And I won't just leave you.'

'I don't need you here. I need to focus on what is about to happen. You are just a distraction.'

He felt an arm on his elbow and he was spun round with more force than he could credit her with.

'How could you say that?' she asked, her voice hoarse. 'I've seen you as many things over the last few years—'

'What? As a criminal?' he demanded, almost afraid of the answer. 'A liar?' he pushed, hurting himself just as much as he was hurting her.

'No. I've seen you as the man who came to me one night, needing nothing more than I was willing to give. The man who was willing to go to prison, even though he knew it was wrong. As the man who showed me that I could reach for the things that I wanted in life, the man who encouraged me to do so.'

Something shone in her eyes, making them bright, making her words batter against the armour he so desperately needed. But he couldn't look at it. Couldn't bear to.

'Well, I'm glad you got something out of it. But it's time for you to leave.'

'I won't.'

'Yes, you will!' he shouted. 'I'm trying to protect you!'

'No, you're not, you're trying to protect yourself. I love you,' she said simply. 'I love you. And I want to be here for you. Please. Let me be.'

Had he even heard her? Had he heard her declaration of love, or had he just chosen to ignore it? 'Dimitri,' she cried.

He shook his head, as if rejecting her, as if refusing to accept her love for him.

'My feelings for my father and my brother made me weak, left me open to...' *to the pain*, he said, concluding the sentence in his head—not ready to admit such a thing to anyone but himself.

'Love isn't a weakness. Love is strength. Let me share that strength with you now,' she pleaded.

'No. You're only saying that because you're so desperate to cling to anyone that won't abandon you, leave you like your father,' he growled.

The hurt in her eyes created a chasm where his heart had used to be.

'If you do this you are no better than my father. You will be making the same mistake he did,' she accused. In an instant, fire whipped up around him, his fury, his helplessness, causing him to lash out with unspeakable anger.

'And what chance did you give your father, Anna? Did you speak to him? Tell him about yourself? No.

You walked away from him without telling him who you really were. You didn't give him a chance because he'd failed at the first hurdle, failed to not instantly recognise you. Just like you failed to really try to tell me about our daughter. Tell me, Anna, is it easy to walk away and blame others for leaving you?'

Pain lashed across her heart as his whip-harsh words rained down upon her. Nausea swelled in her stomach and her head swam. She reached out an arm to steady herself on the table in the kitchen.

'How could you say that?' she demanded.

'Is it not the truth?' he said with a shrug, as if it were simple, as if it were true. Horrified, she pressed a shaking hand to her lips.

'No,' she said, her voice wavering, no longer truly confident of what she had believed her entire life. 'No,' she said with a strength she no longer felt. 'But I will not subject my daughter to this, to you. You want me to protect my child? Then I will,' she said, turning away from him. Turning away from the accusations and the hateful words.

Anna packed with numb fingers. She filled the small suitcase she had brought with her with only the clothes she had come to Greece with. The lavish designer dresses, the trouser suits and glittering jewels lay untouched in the room. She went to the table and picked up the letter she had started to write to Dimitri, to the father of her child. But that man was, and always had been, a figment of her imagination. And she refused to share those thoughts, those words with a man who would turn his back on them. Who would get rid of them if they were an inconvenience.

What was it in her that made people turn their backs on her? She had married Dimitri in order to provide her daughter with someone who wouldn't repeat the same cycle of accidental neglect. But there had been nothing accidental in the words Dimitri had hurled at her that night. Each one calculated to force her from his life. Each one a barb, sticking in her heart, making her wonder if he was right. If all this time it had been she who had walked away.

She had come to Greece with her daughter, and with dreams of Amalia getting to know her family. But now? Dimitri had become her world. The pain she felt eclipsed everything that had come before it. He was sending her away. Having let her into his life, having shown himself to be everything that she had ever needed, he was throwing her away. Even her father had had the decency to remove himself before she could ever know him. But Dimitri had been cruellest of all. He had shown her what her life could really be, full of love, and family…

She put the small number of belongings she had brought with her back into her suitcase and looked around the room, her gaze falling on the passports for her and her daughter almost accusingly. Her heart warred with her head. She wanted to stay. She wanted to be there for Dimitri. Through all the cruel words he had sent her way, she could see the pain and anguish that racked him so fully.

Flora, with tears in her eyes, had told her that the

boat would be coming for her in one hour. So easy, so quick was it for Dimitri to remove her from his presence. Pride told her to leave, that Dimitri had burned his bridges, but her poor heart begged her to stay. Told her that he would change his mind. That he would come after her. But she knew that hope. She had felt that same hope over and over again, with her father, with her mother. It had no place here.

It was only as the private plane taxied on the runway, her daughter safely in the seat beside her, having slept through the whole awful mess, that she realised that Dimitri hadn't come for her. And that he never would.

CHAPTER ELEVEN

Dear Dimitri,
You gave me hope...

ANNA LOOKED OUT at the fields that ran behind the bed and breakfast that had once been her home, remembering that night in Kavala, the words Dimitri had said. *Everything was both the same and different.*

Her mother was in the kitchen with Amalia, and Anna had stepped outside for fresh air. She needed a moment to take it all in. They were selling the place. Her mother, understandably, wanted a fresh start. She needed, they *all* needed, to leave the village that had been so cruel and full of so many painful memories. Her mother had rented a small house by the sea, and some of the money from the sale would provide a strong future there for her.

The day she had met her mother from the institution Mary had asked Anna for her forgiveness. She had said how sorry she was for the weight she had placed on Anna, for the hardness and difficulty she had put upon them. She had spoken of her love for Anna and Amalia, and Anna forgave her completely. They knew that it wouldn't be easy, that her mother was an alcoholic and that there would always be an addiction there, but her mother had promised to do her best to fight for her sobriety every single day. Anna had never seen her mother as strong, but this time she truly felt there was a difference. In the last month, she had seen her mother fight with an energy she had felt missing in herself.

They had spoken about her father and it was difficult for Anna to hear that her mother had felt betrayed when she reached out to her father. That Mary had felt terrified that Anna wouldn't come back, would have chosen the man who had rejected them both, over her. Anna had warred with herself, feeling guilty that she had sought him out, but angry that her mother hadn't been able to understand. At the time. There were hurts on both sides, and they wouldn't just disappear, but they both had to work through them. Her mother's rehabilitation didn't just overwrite all the pains of the past, but they were both willing to try and resolve them now.

But Anna hadn't forgotten the way the ground beneath her had shaken when Dimitri had thrown his hurtful accusations her way. From the moment the words had fallen from his lips, Anna had wondered, chest aching, whether he'd been right.

And deep down, with a very long, very hard look within herself, she realised that he was right.

Yes, her father had left, and there was no denying that. But when she'd gone to London three years before…she had left before she'd given him a chance. And she hated that. Hated both herself and Dimitri for showing her that about herself.

But in the last three weeks she had decided to do something about it.

A week ago she had called the number for the restaurant owned by her father. Although she had warred with the idea of going to London in person, she felt that her first tentative steps towards a relationship with him should be made gently. She had braced herself for all possibilities—rejection, anger, hurt…but she had hoped for love. And this time she had been right. Soon she would arrange a time to go to London and meet her father. But first…

Looking out over the fields, Anna clutched her mobile in a tight fist. For seven days she had tried to reach out to the Sheikh of Ter'harn. She almost laughed at herself. She, speaking to the ruler of a country she hadn't even heard of more than two months ago. Naturally her calls had gone unanswered. Initially. But every day she had called five times, because she needed his help. She honestly didn't think she could put her plan into motion without it, and she refused to drum up some fake injury to Amalia to get Dimitri's attention. So every day she had spoken to the same assistant, but unlike last time she refused to be ignored, dismissed or lied to. Every day the same assistant explained that she couldn't speak to Danyl.

Until today.

* * *

Dimitri ran a hand over his face, his palm passing over what had long stopped being stubble and was now nearly a full beard. He sat heavily down at the wooden table on the patio and looked out to a sea that was about to swallow the sun whole.

He was thankful. The night suited him better ever since Anna and Amalia had left the island.

You loved neither of us enough to sacrifice yourself. His own words had run over and over again in Dimitri's head in the past few weeks. If he'd known how much it would hurt to sacrifice himself, his own feelings, he might have forgiven his father. Might have.

But he needed to remain strong. The media circus that had descended on the Kyriakou Bank had been nothing short of a plague. Ironically it was the fact that he'd been instrumental in bringing down his own father that had allowed the board of governors to stay true and faithful. And if nothing else, the Greeks loved a family tragedy.

Perhaps he had been most surprised by Eleni Kyriakou. She had come to see him and asked for his forgiveness. She hadn't known the actions that her husband had taken, and surprisingly became a bridge between him and the fragmented people that considered themselves his family.

But every time the word 'family' entered his mind, images of Amalia flashed over the pain—Amalia at breakfast throwing food at him, in the pool throwing water at him. But the place he couldn't allow his mind to wander was to Anna. Every time it did, he tried to cling to the old wound of hurt that she had kept her daughter from him, but it wouldn't stick. Because this time it was him, keeping himself from Amalia, from Anna.

He wondered what they were doing now. David had told him about the sale of the B & B. But, aside from the news that her mother was renting a small house by the sea, he knew nothing. And, having experienced life with his daughter, with Anna, he was even more tortured by their absence. By the loss of them.

Two days after they had left, he had finally faced the studio he had created for Anna. He'd been unable to stop himself from entering a place he'd begun to think of as *hers*. Unable to prevent himself from desperately seeking out any remnants of her, a trace of her that showed she hadn't just been a figment of his imagination.

There on the bench had been a completed sculpture. It had stopped him in his tracks, his fingers itching to reach out and caress the smooth lines of the three orbs, linked within a band, a bond, joining the three figures he'd come to imagine were Anna, Amalia and himself.

Over the last three weeks his hands had learned the shape, the feel of the solid fired clay, the silky green-blue glaze that covered it. He had clung to it, almost the same way that Amalia had clung to Anna's first sculpture. The one that had shown him a hint of her hopes and dreams. The ones he'd so very much wanted her to fulfil.

Dimitri heard the door to his house open and close and couldn't even bring himself to find out who had arrived. A bottle of whisky was placed on the table beneath the pergola on the patio and Danyl poured his tall frame into the seat opposite him.

Dimitri scoffed. 'When it was Antonio's turn I brought coffee.'

'Then perhaps it's best that we know what the other needs. Because you're going to need more than coffee.'

'Why are you here?' Dimitri demanded. 'Don't you have a country to run?'

'I do. But friends are more important. You are more important.'

'I'm touched. Deeply. Truly. You can go now,' Dimitri said, reaching out for the bottle of whisky. As if anyone could dismiss a sheikh so easily—as if he could dismiss Danyl so easily.

'Not yet.'

'I'm better off alone,' Dimitri growled.

'You've never been alone, Dimitri—you have me and Antonio.'

'It's different.'

'Why?'

'Because…' He searched for a way to express his feelings without hurting his friend and failed. He could only find an honest reply in the deepest part of his heart and hope that Danyl would understand. 'I could survive without you both. I don't think I could survive if she left me.'

'So you pushed her away?' Danyl asked, no hint

of anger or hurt from Dimitri's easy dismissal of the fellow members of the Winners' Circle.

'I had to. Look at what I did to her, Danyl... Blackmailing her into marriage, holding her and her daughter hostage to my whims. All my talk of protection, and the one person they should have been protected from was me. She is better off without me.'

'I do not believe that. Not for one second. And neither does she.'

Danyl placed a small package on the table, and Dimitri stared at it, frowning at the stack of letters, unable quite yet to reach out and take them. He studied Danyl as he poured two rather unhealthy measures of amber liquid into two glasses and didn't say a word as Danyl placed one in front of him before heading back into the house.

Hesitantly he reached for the small shoebox packed full of letters, each envelope bearing his name, each one headed with a date. He ran his fingers over the fine spines, the last letter dated only weeks before.

'This will take me years,' he tossed over his shoulder to his friend, who had retreated.

Tentatively he reached for the first one, pulling it free from the sealed envelope, and his heart stopped when he read the first line.

Dear Dimitri,
I gave birth to our daughter today and it was the most incredible thing... The moment she was placed in my arms I knew the most over-

whelming kind of love. A love that I never thought was possible. It was full and bright and so very powerful.

Powerful enough, I hope, to help me on this path without you.

The day after you left my bed I read in the newspapers that you had been arrested for fraud. Not just any kind of fraud but stealing millions and millions of dollars from your own business.

I can't imagine how you could have done such a thing. How I could have taken you into my arms, into my bed and even into my heart in such a small space of time. I still can't.

So I'm choosing not to. I'm choosing to write to the man I spent one incredible night with. To share all the wondrous things about our child in letters written not to the man I read about in headlines, plastered there for the world to see, but the man who gave me such pleasure, such joy, and who unknowingly fathered the most precious child with her mop of dark-as-night curly hair and midnight-blue eyes that are far too knowing for one so young.

And it's because of that beautiful little girl that I cannot tell you—the you that was arrested, imprisoned in the last few weeks, the you that was found guilty. How could I expose our daughter to such a man? The you that I write to—and will continue to write to—will understand.

I hope. I feel.

It will not be easy, raising her on my own, with Ma to deal with and the bed and breakfast to manage, but I'll find a way. I have to. Because it isn't just about me any more, or even about you.

It is about our child.

Dear Dimitri,
Today our daughter took her first steps...

Dear Dimitri,
Today was...awful. It's so hard doing this by myself. My mother... No. You don't need to know that. But Amalia—she's growing so strong. Like you, I imagine.

Goosebumps rose on his arms and his heart pounded in his chest as each word echoed in his mind with Anna's voice, the hope, the love, the sadness, the emotions that she had poured into these pages, bringing them to life in his mind for him, despite his absence and despite her doubts of him. He saw each event through her eyes and felt each one through her voice and words. And he realised that she'd always kept him as a part of his daughter's life, even when she'd thought him cruel, even when she thought he'd rejected her, or was unfit to parent Amalia.

Dear Dimitri,
Our daughter has a will of iron! She's refusing

*almost every single piece of food I put in front
of her, apart from hummus and breadsticks!*

Dear Dimitri...

On and on the letters went, filling the gaps in his
experiences, making him laugh with the amusing an-
ecdotes, hurting him with the difficulties she'd gone
through raising their daughter alone. Until he got to
letters that must have been written in Greece, during
her time here. His whole body ached as the words
wrapped vines of love tighter and tighter around his
heart.

Dear Dimitri,
Today I realised that I love you. It's a precious,
powerful love, and one day you'll be ready to
hear it, but I don't think that day is today.

What had he done? He realised with shock that he
didn't want to protect himself any more. If it meant
missing out on all these things, and all there was to
come…he didn't want it. If opening himself to it, if
making himself vulnerable to love meant he got to
experience these incredible moments, these unimagi-
nable feelings, then he'd do it. He didn't want to make
the same mistakes as their fathers. He wanted to love
Anna and Amalia and be stronger for it.

'Danyl? Danyl!' he shouted. 'I have to go to Ireland. Now.'

Danyl stood in the sliding window frames. 'I don't

think that's such a good idea,' his friend said, silhouetted by the light from the house.

'Why not?' Dimitri demanded. 'I have to find Anna. So why the hell wouldn't that be a good idea?' If he was shouting, he didn't care.

'Because,' a voice said from somewhere within the house, 'I'm not in Ireland.'

As Danyl retreated, Anna came forward, and Dimitri's mind went blank. She was a vision, standing there in the light, the way he'd always seen her. The way that he'd always imagined her through those long, dark nights in prison, before he'd allowed the misunderstandings and the hurt to mar her features, his impression of her. The light he had needed in the darkness, the light he still needed.

'Anna...' He stood from the table and went to her. He wanted to take her into his arms, hold her to him and never let her go. But he couldn't. Not yet. He needed to find the words...needed to tell her all that he felt, all that he wanted...all that he loved.

'I pushed you away.'

'Yes, you did,' she said simply. There was no trace of accusation or hurt there, just a statement of fact.

'I pushed you away because I was afraid. I had spent so long being determined that I was better off on my own, that I was the only person who could protect myself. But you—you were trying to protect me from my own darkness, from my own isolation. I let my fear of people betraying me, lying to me, using me—my father, my brother—twist the faith you put into me. The love you gave me. You didn't have to say it, Anna. I saw it there, every time I looked at you. I didn't allow you the chance to tell me, because I was so afraid of it.' She was smiling. Why was she smiling? He had caused her so much hurt, but he had to push on, he had to tell her everything. 'My father's betrayal was the final straw, but instead of seeking comfort from you—a comfort I didn't think I deserved or could even survive—I sent you away. Because truly, deep down, I was worried that I'd never be able to be alone again, never be safe. Because I thought that love threatened that safety. That security. I just didn't realise that you were right. That love is strength, that it makes you able to survive anything.'

She reached out a hand and placed it on his cheek.

'I didn't make it easy on you,' she said gently. 'I have thought a lot about what you said that night—'

'Anna—'

'No, wait. You were right. Partly right,' she conceded. 'I once told you that I'd never forgive you for forcing me to marry you. But I know that it was the only way I could face my issues. So yes, you were right. I would have run, would have hidden, without really knowing it. Without realising. But you showed me what it was that I was doing. Hiding from my hopes and my fears, my father. You. That's why it was so easy for me to believe your assistant. To use that as an excuse not to try harder to tell you about Amalia. About how I felt. Because I fell in love with you one night three years ago. But if you'll have me, I'll love you for ever.'

'You forgive me?' he asked into the night.

'Of course I forgive you. I love you. And that love can never be taken away, or undermined, by anything. I give it to you freely, for the man you really are. Not just the man I met one night three years ago, and not the figment of my imagination that I wrote all those letters to, but you.'

'Mrs Kyriakou,' he said, getting down on one knee on the cold stone floor, ignoring the light laugh that fell from her lips, 'throughout everything you have been the one person to see me, when I couldn't even see myself. You are kind, generous, loving and, more than anything, so incredibly strong. I am humbled by you. Will you do me the honour of becoming my wife?'

'I'm already your wife, Dimitri,' Anna said, laughter and love shining bright in her beautiful eyes.

'I want to do it properly this time. With your friends and family, with mine. All of us. Not alone any more, but together.'

Anna had barely said yes, when Dimitri pulled her towards him as his lips crashed down against hers. For Anna it was the best kiss she'd had, and would ever receive.

EPILOGUE

Dear Amalia,
Today was a very special day. It was your fifth
birthday. Of course, you clearly enjoyed the cake
more than the presents. I think you might be a
chef when you grow up. But whether you are a
chef, a scientist, a politician or an astronaut—
the last being your current chosen career path—
you are perfect in every way. Watching you grow
into a strong, quite often determined and always
very loud little lady has been one of the greatest
pleasures in my life so far.

Your uncles Antonio and Danyl and their
partners flew in to join us and you announced
your expectations of cousins quite forcefully.
Once I considered them friends but, Amalia,
it was you who made us all a family.

Today—as a family—we had an extra pres-
ent for your birthday. You won't remember this,
but you ran around the house for almost forty
minutes, screaming with joy at the prospect of
a little brother or sister to boss around. You

*explained in quite some detail about your plans
for our new family member, who will arrive in
six months' time, and announced that it wasn't
long enough to do all the things that needed
to be done. And then you demanded ice cream
because you were going to be the best older
sister that anyone ever had. And I believe you.*

*Today, Amalia, you showed me once again
the incredible unconditional love that runs in
the women of our family. The men—if we're
having a boy!—will have a lot to live up to, and
we'll try every single day to do so.*
All my love, special girl,
Your father

As DIMITRI PLACED the letter into the envelope, Anna
walked into their bedroom, the silk nightdress showing the small bump that was to be their next child.
He rose and placed a hand on the curve of her abdo-
men, marvelling at the miracle of it.

'Eyes up, Mr Kyriakou—there'll be plenty of time
for you to indulge in our pregnancy. And I know
that in a few months' time, you'll barely spare me
a glance. So I'm going to take all you can give me
for now.'

'I assure you that won't be a problem. How could
I ever take you for granted?' he said, smiling down
at the incredible woman that was his wife.

They had renewed their vows almost three years
ago to the day, and every day since they had remade
those promises, they had spoken words of love,

written them, committed them to paper. They documented both the good days and the hard days, but there had never been bad days. They had books full of notes and letters describing their love and their joy, books that would continue to be filled until their last days.

* * * * *

If you enjoyed
Claimed for the Greek's Child
you're sure to enjoy these other stories
by Pippa Roscoe!

Conquering His Virgin Queen
A Ring to Take His Revenge

Available now!

COMING NEXT MONTH FROM

HARLEQUIN

Presents.®

Available March 19, 2019

#3705 THE ITALIAN DEMANDS HIS HEIRS
Billionaires at the Altar
by Lynne Graham
To counter a media scandal, Raffaele must marry Vivi. And he's not above using seduction to convince her! But when Vivi discovers she's pregnant, Raffaele demands she meet him down the aisle—for real!

#3706 THE SICILIAN'S SECRET SON
Secret Heirs of Billionaires
by Angela Bissell
When Luca uncovers the existence of his hidden son, he's determined to whisk his new family away to his Sicilian estate. But Luca knows there's only one way to truly claim Annah and his son—marriage!

#3707 INNOCENT'S NINE-MONTH SCANDAL
One Night With Consequences
by Dani Collins
When Rozalia appears on Viktor's doorstep, his world is thrown into chaos! But their passion has consequences...and Viktor refuses to let scandal ruin his family. Their baby will be legitimate! And Rozi? She will be his...

#3708 CHOSEN AS THE SHEIKH'S ROYAL BRIDE
Conveniently Wed!
by Jennie Lucas
Beth can hardly believe Sheikh Omar would even notice her. So when she's chosen as his bride, she's stunned. Thrown into a world of unimagined luxury, can this shy Cinderella ever be a queen?

HPCNM0319RA

#3709 SPANIARD'S BABY OF REVENGE
by Clare Connelly
Antonio plans to persuade innocent Amelia to sell her shares in his rival's business. But he doesn't plan on their intense connection—and is stunned to discover their nine-month consequence. To secure his child, he'll make Amelia his wife!

#3710 CLAIMING MY UNTOUCHED MISTRESS
by Heidi Rice
Edie agreed to clear her family's debts by posing as my temporary mistress, helping expose my business rivals. Yet Edie's innocence is a temptation I couldn't have imagined. Our chemistry is spectacular—now I'll claim Edie for more than pleasure!

#3711 REUNITED BY A SHOCK PREGNANCY
by Chantelle Shaw
Sienna should not be secretly attending her ex-husband's wedding. Until she realizes Nico isn't the groom... But when he follows her, their burning fire reignites, leaving Sienna shockingly pregnant with the Italian's child!

#3712 THE BILLIONAIRE'S VIRGIN TEMPTATION
by Michelle Conder
Ruby is stunned when Sam sweeps her into an anonymous seduction! But when Ruby realizes Sam is her new boss, and they're left stranded together, his forbidden touch could be powerful enough to unravel Ruby forever...

YOU CAN FIND MORE INFORMATION ON UPCOMING HARLEQUIN® TITLES, FREE EXCERPTS AND MORE AT WWW.HARLEQUIN.COM.

HPCNM0319RB

Get 4 FREE REWARDS!

We'll send you 2 FREE Books
plus 2 FREE Mystery Gifts.

Harlequin Presents® books feature a sensational and sophisticated world of international romance where sinfully tempting heroes ignite passion.

FREE
Value Over
$20

YES! Please send me 2 FREE Harlequin Presents® novels and my 2 FREE gifts (gifts are worth about $10 retail). After receiving them, if I don't wish to receive any more books, I can return the shipping statement marked "cancel." If I don't cancel, I will receive 6 brand-new novels every month and be billed just $4.55 each for the regular-print edition or $5.55 each for the larger-print edition in the U.S., or $5.49 each for the regular-print edition or $5.99 each for the larger-print edition in Canada. That's a savings of at least 11% off the cover price! It's quite a bargain! Shipping and handling is just 50¢ per book in the U.S. and 75¢ per book in Canada.* I understand that accepting the 2 free books and gifts places me under no obligation to buy anything. I can always return a shipment and cancel at any time. The free books and gifts are mine to keep no matter what I decide.

Choose one: ☐ **Harlequin Presents®**
Regular-Print
(106/306 HDN GMYX)

☐ **Harlequin Presents®**
Larger-Print
(176/376 HDN GMYX)

Name (please print)

Address   Apt. #

City   State/Province   Zip/Postal Code

Mail to the **Reader Service:**
IN U.S.A.: P.O. Box 1341, Buffalo, NY 14240-8531
IN CANADA: P.O. Box 603, Fort Erie, Ontario L2A 5X3

Want to try 2 free books from another series! Call 1-800-873-8635 or visit www.ReaderService.com.

*Terms and prices subject to change without notice. Prices do not include sales taxes, which will be charged (if applicable) based on your state or country of residence. Canadian residents will be charged applicable taxes. Offer not valid in Quebec. This offer is limited to one order per household. Books received may not be as shown. Not valid for current subscribers to Harlequin Presents books. All orders subject to approval. Credit or debit balances in a customer's account(s) may be offset by any other outstanding balance owed by or to the customer. Please allow 4 to 6 weeks for delivery. Offer available while quantities last.

Your Privacy—The Reader Service is committed to protecting your privacy. Our Privacy Policy is available online at www.ReaderService.com or upon request from the Reader Service. We make a portion of our mailing list available to reputable third parties that offer products we believe may interest you. If you prefer that we not exchange your name with third parties, or if you wish to clarify or modify your communication preferences, please visit us at www.ReaderService.com/consumerschoice or write to us at Reader Service Preference Service, P.O. Box 9062, Buffalo, NY 14240-9062. Include your complete name and address.

HP19R

SPECIAL EXCERPT FROM

*Walking into my casino, Edie Spencer seemed like a
spoiled heiress—until she agreed to clear her family's
debts by posing as my temporary mistress. My plan? To
use her to expose my business rivals. Yet discovering
Edie's innocence has led to greater temptation than I
could have imagined. Our chemistry is spectacular—
now I'll claim Edie for so much more than pleasure!*

*Read on for a sneak preview of
Heidi Rice's next story,*
Claiming My Untouched Mistress.

"Your sister told me exactly how deep your financial troubles go,"
I said. "I have a possible solution."

"What is it?" Edie said, desperation plain on her face.

"Would you consider working for me?" I asked.

"You're…you're offering me a job?"

She sounded so surprised, I found my lips curving in amusement
again.

"As it happens, I am hosting an event at my new estate near
Nice at the end of the month. I could use your skills as part of the
team I'm putting together."

"What exactly do you need me to do?" she said, her eagerness
a sop to my ego.

"The guests I am inviting are some of the world's most powerful
businessmen and women." I outlined the job. "They have all shown
an interest in investing in the expansion of the Allegri brand. The
event is a way of assessing their suitability as investors. As part of
the week, I will be offering some recreational poker events. These

people are highly competitive and they enjoy games of chance. What they don't know is that how they play poker tells me a great deal more about their personalities and their business acumen— and whether we will be compatible—than a simple profit-and-loss portfolio of their companies. But I find that successful people, no matter how competitive they are, are also smart enough to know that they cannot best me at a poker table. So I need someone who does not intimidate them, but who can observe how they play and make those assessments for me." I kept my eyes on her reaction, surprised myself by how much I wanted her to say yes.

My attraction to her might be unexpected, but I had spent a lifetime living by my wits and never doubting my instincts. When I had originally considered giving her a hosting position I'd been aware of the possible fringe benefits for both of us and I didn't see why that should change. She had made it very clear she was more than happy to blur the lines between employer and lover, and all her responses made it equally clear she desired me as much as I desired her.

"I'll pay you four thousand euros for the fortnight," I said, to make her position clear. This was a genuine job, and a job she would be very good at. "Joe can brief you on each of the participants— and what I need to know about them. If you do a good enough job, and your skills prove as useful as I'm expecting them to be, I would consider offering you a probationary position."

She blinked several times, her skin now flushed a dark pink, but didn't say anything.

"So do you want the job?" I asked, letting my impatience show, annoyed by the strange feeling of anticipation. Why should it matter to me if she declined my offer?

"Yes, yes," she said. "I'll take the job."

Don't miss
Claiming My Untouched Mistress.
Available April 2019 wherever
Harlequin® Presents books and ebooks are sold.

www.Harlequin.com

Copyright © 2019 by Heidi Rice

HPEXP0319

HARLEQUIN

Presents®

Coming next month—
a captivating tale of innocence and desire!

In *Innocent's Nine-Month Scandal*, Rozi finds herself
in Budapest, searching for a beloved family heirloom.
But when the search takes her to billionaire Viktor's
door, she's shocked by their red-hot attraction…and the
consequences of their passion are even more shocking!

Control is *everything* to billionaire Viktor Rohan. Then
Rozalia Toth appears on his mansion's doorstep, looking
for a family heirloom, and throws his world into chaos!
Her sweetness intrigues him beyond measure…and as
their inescapable chemistry explodes, Viktor realizes Rozi's
innocence isn't an act. But their passion has consequences, and
Viktor refuses to let scandal ruin his family again. Their baby
will be legitimate! And Rozi? She will be his…

Innocent's Nine-Month Scandal

One Night With Consequences

Available April 2019

HPBPA0319

Want to give in to temptation with steamy tales of irresistible desire?

Check out **Harlequin® Presents®**, **Harlequin® Desire** and **Harlequin® Kimani™ Romance** books!

New books available every month!

CONNECT WITH US AT:

Facebook.com/groups/HarlequinConnection

 Facebook.com/HarlequinBooks

 Twitter.com/HarlequinBooks

 Instagram.com/HarlequinBooks

 Pinterest.com/HarlequinBooks

ReaderService.com

HARLEQUIN®

ROMANCE WHEN YOU NEED IT

PGENRE2018